The Georgellen Club

Mike Keenan

The Georgellen Club

Author: Mike Keenan

Printed in the United States

Published 2017, First Look Publishing (Austin)

Version 1.0

ISBN: 978-0-9913907-8-6 (paper)

      978-0-9913907-9-3 (digital)

Cover Photo: Nancy Smith

Cover Graphic: Brian Burrowes

Printed by CreateSpace, a DBA of On-Demand

Publishing, LLC

To my lovely wife Ann,
my close friends, Andrea and Nancy,
my family, and, of course, LOS MEYERLANDOS.

GEORGELLEN CLUB

The Owner

I murdered a man. I didn't do it with my own hands. I paid someone to do it. I put it into motion. In the words of Tommy Aquinas, I was the "prime mover." And I have no regrets about my sin. The man who was murdered had it coming. He had done enough damage. If you are interested, here is my story.

I graduated from high school ambitionless. College was within reach, none of the elite institutions, but somewhere. However, I hated school. I saw no point in it, which may have been a mistake on my part. I considered the army, but I knew that discipline and I were not compatible. My dad, a car salesman, made it clear to me I had to do something, if not school, or the military, then a job.

I wasted three years. I lived at home and tried a series of menial jobs. I looked in the newspaper. There were ads for delivery boys and phone solicitors. I tried a few. I worked at a car wash. I parked cars. I drove a cab. I sold cutlery (which lasted one week.) I refer to those years as my *period of doing nothing.*

One evening, my father away selling the cars that would

fill my belly, I saw an ad on television. It was local variety, a thirty second clip that appealed to me. It seemed promising and, if nothing else, would get my parents off my back. I enrolled in the Night Owl School of Bartending.

Six weeks later I came out a bartender. It cost me three hundred dollars. (It cost my dad three hundred dollars.) I learned the art of mixology. Night Owl placed me into my first job as a bartender. I moved out of my parents' house and that's when I met the man I murdered.

I went to work at Woodley's, a bar restaurant in southwest Houston. It was a big bright place. The manager was easy to work for. It was in a strip center that's run down now. Woodley's is long gone. Last I looked the Woodley's space had been converted into a pawnshop and a convenience store.

I met Carter McCrae at Woodley's. We hit it off. He was a year older than me. We tended bar together. He showed me the ropes. We decided to room together. I'd been living in a one bedroom apartment a short drive from Woodley's. (I bought a used car from my dad.) Carter and I rented a house in Bellaire which is its own city engulfed by greater Houston.

Carter was a charming, good-looking guy who introduced me to the world of excess. He was a chick magnet. I was not. I watched with fascination as he picked up women and scored with them on a steady basis. It amazed me how he never seemed worried that a former conquest might drop in while he was engaged in his latest conjugation. But he had a basic understanding of people and upon reflection the bar material he was picking up was of the one night variety so there must have been a mutual understanding that come daylight both parties would go their separate ways.

I saw Carter McCrae change. The river of women who rolled through our rent house during the two years Carter and I lived together were all easy lookers. I didn't see any super models but they were all well above average. I was eating breakfast one morning (Woodley's was a night time gig) when a tall blond girl came out of Carter's room on her way out. She was nice. She shook hands with me. We actually chatted for a few minutes. Unlike the other women Carter seduced, this girl was a little on the plain side. (I'm being generous.) Just as we'd finished our conversation a brief look passed over her face. She excused herself and walked back to Carter's bedroom, fumbling with her purse as she pulled out a cluster of twenty dollar bills. And that is where it began for Carter.

It went on for about a year. The volume of women slowed down to what appeared to be a manageable clientele. Most were well dressed and, judging from their looks, undoubtedly lonely. I wish to be clear. Carter and I were not friends. Our relationship was strictly that of roommates. In defence of him, he was very responsible with money. He always came up with his half of the rent and bills on time. I never once had to remind him it was the first of the month. I didn't judge him at first. But I did not want an association with a male hooker. He eventually came to me and announced he was quitting Woodley's and moving out. He didn't tell me what he was going to do, but I gathered he was entering the big leagues of money for sex.

That was okay by me. I was making good money at Woodley's. I knew I could cover expenses by myself until I found another roommate. I was satisfied where I was. I'd been at Woodley's two years, my longest time on a job. I liked my boss, and I liked the foothold I'd gotten in life.

A week after he moved out, Carter called me. He had forgotten a picture of the Grand Canyon on a bookcase in his room. I knew the picture and knew how much Carter liked it. He pulled up in a brand new black Mercedes sedan. Carter had owned an old Ford pickup. The Mercedes caught me off guard. Before he could come in, I walked out onto the driveway. I held the picture. He rolled down the car window. On the passenger side was a woman at least twenty years older than Carter. He introduced her as Peggy Bosh. She, like the other recent women in Carter's life, was, to be frank, rather unattractive. To my surprise, Carter introduced her as his fiancé. She smiled. I reached across Carter and shook her hand. We spent a few minutes engaged in small talk. Carter thanked me for the picture. He suggested to Peggy Bosh that the Grand Canyon would be a good honeymoon spot. His fiancé invited me to the wedding when they set a date. I accepted but made no special note to myself about it. They drove off.

I kept an eye on the wedding announcements. I figured, surely, Peggy Bosh would see through Carter McCrae. But, no, lonely people are either very hard or very malleable. A month later I found their wedding announcement. Peggy Bosh looked happy. I felt sorry for her. I didn't know her and probably shouldn't have cared one way or another but I could see all that joy etched on her face coming to an end. Carter had no conscience about taking advantage of that lonely woman.

I continued working at Woodley's. The place was hopping. Periodically, women would ask me what Carter was up to. I hadn't found a roommate. I was careful about finding another. I found living by myself enjoyable. And I was making ends meet.

A man walked up to me one night. I was behind the bar. He introduced himself as George Jax. He looked about fifty years old, short, with big forearms, a damaged left hand that was partially missing, and thinning grey hair. I imagined him wearing a hard hat and holding a hammer. But he was no construction worker. No indeed. He cut straight to the point and asked me if I would consider changing jobs. It turned out he owned five bar restaurants, all of them spaced along Interstate 45. He had frequented Woodley's both as a patron who liked good food and liquor, but also as a competitor keeping an eye out for ideas and people. He had been watching me for several months. He liked my style, my rapport with people.

I agreed to meet him on Wednesday, my day off. He took me on a driving tour of his five bar eateries. All were first rate. One was north of Houston near the airport. One sat inside Loop 610. The remaining three were along South Interstate 45, known as the Gulf Freeway, with the last of them, the Georgellen Club, resting in Galveston overlooking the Gulf of Mexico.

I listened to his pitch. He wanted me to manage the bar at the Georgellen Club, and, if things worked out, someday the entire restaurant. It was a big move for me. I felt a touch of loyalty toward Woodley's. But I knew by then that life was motion, either forward, or backwards. I accepted his offer. I gave a week's notice at Woodley's, and then went to work for George Jax.

I was a natural at managing the bar. Not only was I an experienced bartender by now, but I quickly developed a good relationship with the staff. I set schedules, counted cash at day's end, ordered inventory, and, if I must say so, had the bar running like a top. George Jax liked me. Going to work for him was a good idea.

George Jax was a talker. He confided in me things that I would not have expected. Perhaps he was an open book with everyone. He was a widower. His wife, Ellen, died leaving him with a daughter, Julia. When I went to work for him, she was a sophomore in a private high school on the Island. I met her a few times. She was pretty, but not beautiful, a quiet, obedient girl who her father loved and who he raised with a series of well vetted nannies.

He owned two homes, one in Conroe, Texas, north of Houston, and the other on Galveston Island proper. Both were nice homes. Julia lived in the Galveston home, walking distance from her school. A typical week for George Jax would have him leave his Conroe home, where he had spent the previous night, then drive south on Interstate 45, stopping for an hour or two at each of his five restaurants. By late afternoon he would be at the Georgellen Club where he would have a drink then go home to his daughter for an evening meal. A day or two spent in Galveston, he would then make the same trip, in reverse, back to Conroe, once again stopping at each restaurant. He was successful, self made and loved life second only to his daughter.

It was on one of those stops at the Georgellen Club that George Jax became not only indebted to me, but somewhat of a surrogate father as well. He and I were in the Georgellen Club, me behind the bar, when he clutched his chest, sank to one knee, then rolled over on the floor. I recognized this as a heart attack and administered CPR, one of the few meaningful things I picked up in that blur of menial jobs I had yawned through in my past. I kept him alive, clumsily I admit, until an EMS team arrived and stabilized him. They rushed him to John Sealy Hospital where he underwent bypass surgery to three of his coronary arteries. He lived and recovered fully. He lost weight, stopped smoking, and began walking on the beach. From my station behind the bar I often saw father and daughter walking in the sand, waves of salt water licking at their bare feet.

In my mind, he owed me nothing. But he was grateful, extremely so. He approached me a year or so after the heart attack, looking somewhat sheepish. He was a bold fellow who didn't mince words, and the few times I had seen him employ tact had come across as clumsy. He hemmed and hawed a bit with me then asked would I become his daughter's godfather, not in the legal sense, but would I look out for her? And would I become trustee of the trust he was setting up for her benefit? His brush with death had impressed upon him the need for his daughter's financial security. He had no one to turn to, no immediate family, and his wife's brother, uncle to Julia, had not been heard from in years.

I didn't deliberate. I took on the task, yes, for the salary the trusteeship would pay, but primarily because I liked George

Jax and fully appreciated what he had done for me. We shook hands. That was our contract. That was all we needed. He was the real deal and I committed to become as much. He died five years later. The heart finally wore out. His funeral was simple. He had few friends. He was uneasy with most people. I received a notice in the mail from his lawyer requesting my presence at the reading of his will where my role as trustee was confirmed and, as George had promised, I was left the Georgellen Club.

I ran the club as though George Jax still owned it and might walk in at any minute. I wanted it to be a monument to the man. And I accepted my role as trustee with the highest degree of responsibility. From George's attorney I learned that as trustee I had broad powers. With much deliberation, I sold the other four establishments along with the Conroe home, investing the proceeds of those sales for the benefit of his daughter. The investments grew significantly. I knew that George's main desire was the health and safety and happiness of his daughter, and that liquidating those properties would be fine. The trust paid income to Julia for life, with any amount left over at her death going to a series of charities unless she designated someone in her Will to receive the remnant. At age forty-five, if she desired, she could also have me removed as trustee and designate someone, other than herself, as the successor trustee.

I got along reasonably well with Julia. It dawned on her that she had more money than she could ever spend. She lived in the house she and her father had occupied in Galveston. I think she appreciated that her father was looking out for her by appointing me, not only as trustee, but also as an informal guardian. She had authority issues, but we managed to work through those. She had not graduated college, but had lived the life of a student, until finally giving up the idea. When she turned twenty-one, according to the terms of the trust, I was instructed to give her an allowance of five thousand dollars a month, an amount free and clear of utilities and taxes on the home she lived in. I paid those amounts regularly from the trust, receiving the bills directly at my office. At age thirty-five the trust raised her amount of monthly income to ten thousand dollars with the opportunity to increase that amount in the sole discretion of the trustee. With no living expenses beyond groceries and gas for her car (leased by the trust) she had no incentive to do much other than party. George Jax was a tough, hard businessman, but if he liked you, (as he did me) he was quite generous. And he had no problem spoiling Julia from the grave.

Ten years into my role as trustee, Julia was in a car accident, an event that resulted in my becoming more watchful of her. I felt that I had let George Jax down and personally vowed to do a better job, even if it meant exercising some control in her personal life. She was hit broadside, at an intersection in Houston, the outcome of a late night of bacchanalia. Though she survived, she was left with a permanent limp in her right leg and a scar that, after several plastic surgeries, removed damaged tissue from her face leaving her forehead and left cheek noticeably puffy. In her mind's eye, she was disfigured. She became reclusive. Like her father, she was not a natural for making close friends. Her loss of what modest self-esteem she had did not help. She turned away from people, keeping a pair of pit bull dogs as her companions.

Ten more years went by without, other than replacing deceased canines, much change in her reclusion. In that respect, her adoption of a quiet life made mine easier. I suspected she was marking time until she could remove me as trustee. I was fifty-two and she was creeping up on forty-five when he walked into the Georgellen Club.

Carter McCrae was still Carter McCrae. He was heavier, about twenty pounds, and his hair and beard had been artificially darkened, but there was no mistaking the man.

My appearance, on the other hand, had changed substantially. I'm usually the tallest person in the room (six foot, five inches barefoot), but when I roomed with Carter I was thin as a rail. Over the years I had filled out, a good portion of it from weight lifting, and due to the graying then ultimate loss of my red hair, my head was now shaved cleanly bald. Add to that the horned rimmed glasses I had been wearing most of the last decade and I looked completely different than I did thirty years earlier.

Despite my ownership of the club, I was not above jumping behind the bar to wait on patrons. Eventually, Carter ambled up to the bar. He had navigated the room with the same charm as his younger version. He was skilled, energetic, and, not surprisingly, gravitated toward those women who appeared most susceptible to attention. I issued no greeting to him above and beyond what any bartender would. He was friendly. He ordered a glass of red wine. He talked freely. I listened. He was new to Galveston. He liked the Island and wanted to make it home. He had been, among his other professions, a bartender. Did the Georgellen Club have an opening? I told him "no" and could not tell him who on the Island was hiring. At no time in our conversation did I identify myself. Undaunted, he faded into the evening.

I didn't see him for several weeks. I hoped he might have moved on. Then, one night, my worst fear came true. He appeared in the Georgellen Club with Julia Jax in tow. How that union came about I did not know but it didn't surprise me. He had a predatory instinct for Julia's type of woman, someone well dressed who carried herself as the wealthy do, but whose station in life could not disguise a deep reservoir of self-loathing.

They didn't approach the bar. Carter ordered dinner and drinks from their table. I was sure by now that Julia had told him her story and the role the Georgellen Club played in it. When she did venture out, she came to the Georgellen Club where she ate and drank for free. Carter McCrae was on his game.

Over the years I had stayed in touch with Julia Jax

through monthly luncheons. We would visit. I would listen. Whenever I sensed her life going astray I would hire a private investigator to keep me up on her behaviour. At first I think she regarded me as an uncle figure, but as she grew older and more cynical, frustrated by her limp and deteriorating looks, she came to resent me.

I called her and requested that we meet. I suggested lunch, or my office, but she insisted that I come to her house. To my relief, Carter McCrae was not there. We sat on a sunny patio, in lawn chairs, graced by a cool March breeze under a clear blue sky. Life, were it measured in meteorological terms, couldn't get better. Flanking her were her most recent canines of choice, a pair of pit bulls I was certain would, on command, attack anyone who threatened Julia.

I told her all about Carter McCrae. I held nothing back. Of course, she didn't believe me. Carter and she were to be married, sooner rather than later. She appreciated my loyalty to her father, as well as the work I had done as trustee, but she confirmed that I would, in fact, be replaced when she turned forty-five.

"With Carter, presumably" I stated.

She didn't like that remark. Her facial expression said as much. The pit on her right emitted a low, guttural growl and I knew it was time to leave.

It didn't surprise me to see Carter McCrae show up at the Georgellen Club. Instead of working the crowd, he came directly to the bar.

"I thought I recognized you," he said.

"I know what you're up to," I answered.

"Don't get in my way," he said.

I looked him directly in the eye. "I can't prevent Julia from removing me as trustee" I said "but I'll do what I must to keep you from replacing me. As we speak I have an investigator reconstructing your life, every second of it, from the day I met

Peggy Bosh forward. I assume she's still alive?"

"I know people," said Carter. "Don't mess with this."

"You'll never control that girl's money," I assured.

He shrugged and walked away. "We'll see," he said.

That did it for me, the "we'll see" part. Had he mentioned he loved Julia, or that his past was not his present, I might have let it go. "We'll see." I made a phone call to Phil Lugo.

Phil and I went back a long ways. We both survived the Catholic educational system, from the same elementary school to the same high school. Phil's family was a testament to marital strength. His mother was a devout Catholic and his father an avowed atheist. Phil went through Catholic school at the insistence of his mother. His father was a mild fellow who simply held no belief in a deity. Phil professed his atheism in the eighth grade, not in a militant way, but when asked, he was honest. I'm sure he endured the dogma, despite his nonbelief in anything other than the temporal, for his mother's sake. The good nuns, and the priests thereafter, I suspect deemed the salvation of his jeopardized soul their very reason for being. He and I, close as boys, were on a first name basis whenever we saw each other. But that was rare. I never attended high school reunions and, but for one occasion when he came into Woodley's and another time at the shopping mall, I hadn't seen him in most of thirty years. He was always quiet, avoiding attention, and I, not having had the chance to share with him an honest exchange of world views, figured him steadfast in his atheism.

Over the years, I had heard things about Phil, rumors, bartender talk, grapevine whispers about dark deeds, no room for God in Phil's world.

He and I met at the Houston Zoo on a Wednesday, midafternoon, in front of the monkey cage, its inhabitants screeching without cessation.

"You're sure you want to do this, Tommy?"

I nodded.

"Because when you walk through this door, there's no coming back."

"Phil, I've considered that," I said.

"Tommy, this is serious stuff you're playing with. You should take a day or two to think about this."

"I've thought about it," I said.

"Ok," he said, "but after today, its business and not friendship between us. Are we clear?"

Things were to go as follows: In Wharton, Texas, near Houston, on an obscure county road, sat an abandoned barn. By noon three days from now, I would place a backpack with fifty thousand dollars (in one hundred dollar bills) under a pair of boards at the back of that barn. I would never speak, under any circumstances, about this matter again. If I broke confidentiality, my life became expendable. Two Sundays from now, I would be in my office between 8:00 a.m. and noon. Sometime within that window the phone would ring three times. I would not answer it. Three rings would mean that Carter McCrae would not be seen again.

I considered the prospect of being played the fool. Perhaps Phil Lugo would simply keep the money. Or perhaps the mere threat of harm would send Carter scurrying out of Galveston. I could live with that outcome provided he left Julia Jax alone. I debated contacting Phil and having him deliver a forceful message to Carter McCrae as an alternative to murder. But I took Phil's admonition about silence seriously. I trusted Phil, never one to bullshit, to execute the deal as agreed.

I delivered the money. Getting it was no problem. I kept that much and more in my office safe. The drive to Wharton and the placement of the money in the barn went smoothly, but I was looking over my shoulder the entire time. The barn smelled like stale dung, and I wondered if the open fields along the county road might be where Carter McCrae would spend eternity.

Two Sundays later I was in my office before eight

working over the club's books. I pondered the ethics in what I had done. I felt nothing. At 9:45 a.m. the phone on my desk rang. I let it ring once, then twice, then three times. It didn't ring again. I surmised the world had become a better place.

Now, the obvious question: Would a man have another man killed over a mere promise made to a benefactor? The following anecdote might lend some clarity to this inquiry. When I was thirteen, my family took a vacation to a small fishing village on the Gulf Coast. My parents had stumbled upon it several years before. Because my dad sold cars, he had no paid vacation. When he took off from work, it not only dented his wallet, but it cost him in car sales as well. Our vacations were brief (three days including Sunday) and always nearby. It was Saturday, and not much was going on. We were in a small, family-run motel near the beach. My dad was watching a ball game, my mother reading the newspaper, resting as they deserved. Bored, I took a walk along the beach.

Ten minutes into the walk, I came upon a jetty that ran two hundred yards out into the water. There was a group of ten or more people at the end of the jetty pointing furiously at the water. Curiosity got the better of me. I walked out onto the jetty, hopping from boulder to boulder, water lapping on the rocks. When I arrived, I saw that the group was fascinated by a huge hammerhead shark, at least ten feet long, attracted by bait the fishermen in the group were tossing in the water. Within the group, probably drawn by curiosity as well, was a man with a young boy, no more than five years old. The man and the boy, who I assumed to be his son, were equally enthralled by the shark, both of them standing at the water's edge. Suddenly a wave jumped up and sucked the boy into the water not twenty feet from the hungry jaws. The man reacted quickly, pulling the boy, by the arm, up from the water, just ahead of the interested shark. Later, as I walked back to the motel, I reflected on what I had seen. Had the man hesitated at all, the boy would have, no doubt, been hustled out to sea and devoured by the great fish. The horror of it all appealed to me. That was troubling at first. I wanted to dismiss it as a passing aberration. But it has never gone away. There was part of me that wanted to see that big fellow eat.

The Ball Player

I took a fastball in the face while I was playing for Raleigh in the Carolina League. I had aspirations of making it to the majors but that dream died when the Charlotte pitcher, a monster of a guy named Dolph Hurley, threw high and tight. He had a reputation for throwing at people and I guess he earned it. I went down on my knees and watched home plate turn red. Plastic surgery and dental work healed my face, but my left eye had a blind spot. I wasn't the same. Pitchers figured me out. I lost my guts for waiting on a curve ball. I was cut from the parent club, and, after kicking around in the beer leagues for three more years, called it quits.

I moped around feeling sorry for myself for six months. I knew I had to do something. I thought about coaching but the high school or college level required a teaching degree. I considered a coaching career in pro ball but I was twenty-eight years old and, if I couldn't play the game, I didn't want to watch from the dugout. I was born to compete on the field.

I caught a break from Antonio Giannis, a high school buddy of mine. He called me out of the blue. I was working at a convenience store, bored to death. He and I had played ball together growing up, in the kid leagues and in high school. He was a decent player with a good arm but a career in baseball was out of his reach and he knew it. He'd heard what happened to me and that things were going rough.

There I was on my day off, sitting in my apartment, when the phone rang. He and I spent thirty minutes or so rehashing glory days. Eventually he got around to telling me why he had called. He was a liquor salesman. He'd quit college, which he knew wasn't for him, to take a job with Century Beverage and had done quite well. Century was hiring, he was in good with the higher ups, and did I want him to see what he could do for me?

"You mean as a salesman?" I asked.

"Yes," he answered.

"But I've never sold," I said.

"Kenny, tell me what you've got to lose," was his response.

So I went to work for Century. Antonio was right; I had nothing to lose. I told him I owed him big time. He told me it was nothing; he and I were pals. Century hooked me up with an older black man, Luther Jones, as my mentor. Luther taught me a lot. He was retiring in a year or so and Century was looking for his successor. He was very loyal to Century, the company had given him a career, and he vowed not to leave without the transition being seamless. If I proved myself a good fit, I couldn't ask for a better job.

At first I was miserable. I had no selling instincts. Luther was patient. His route ran from Pasadena on the east side of Loop 610, west all the way to Sugarland, and south to the Gulf of Mexico. We'd be driving his route and he'd point to a competitor's salesman driving the same area and say "They'd all love to be where I am and if you learn this business they'll all feel the same way about you."

That appealed to my competitive streak and I got steadily better. Luther had two hundred liquor stores on his route. He knew every owner by his or her first name. He dressed well, always in a fresh suit and tie, his wingtips polished, his hair cut regularly, his nails manicured.

"Don't ever take your grooming for granted," he warned. "This is a professional job. Keep your standards high."

A year later, Luther retired. He deemed me ready. I took over his route and I let neither him nor Century down. I knew every liquor store on that route, every owner on that route, and I dressed as impeccably as Luther had directed. I worked hard and considered that area south of the Loop, east to west and all the way to the Gulf of Mexico, as mine.

I never forgot baseball, its feel, the smell of oil in the palm of your glove. I stayed away from the game intentionally. I missed it, and the one ball game I attended gave me an anxiety attack. I limited my exposure to baseball by reading the sports page, particularly the box scores. I knew who was doing what in print.

I did things pretty much the way Luther did. By that I mean I pushed hard Monday through Thursday to get most of my route out of the way. I'd hit fifty stores a week, averaging twelve to fifteen stores a day. It was my routine to stop in a liquor store, greet the owner (in the small liquor stores the owner usually manned the counter during the day, turning the night shift over to the hired help), and then have him place his order with me. It was all based on quality of product (and Century handled all the name brands) as well as service. Century's delivery trucks were always on time with the order and never left an owner in the lurch. That owner wants his store full of product on weekends and holidays and God help you if your deliveryman doesn't come through. At first the owners were a bit skeptical of me, having relied on Luther all those years. But with Luther's assurance to them that I would be as good to them as he was, and with me making good on Luther's endorsement, the people on my route came to like and respect me.

On Fridays, if I got my route done Monday through Thursday as planned, I'd hit two or three stores in the morning, then take Friday afternoons off. That was nice. It gave me a two and one half day weekend. I had an apartment in Southwest Houston, a stone's throw from Loop 610 that allowed me easy access to anywhere in town including my route.

I was killing a little time on one of those Fridays when I stopped into an athletic complex not far from my apartment. It had been there for several years and I had been tempted to stop in and watch people take batting practice in any one of the twenty batting cages that formed a portion of the complex. There was a driving range, a go cart track, and an indoor shooting range in addition to the batting cages. The cages sat side by side made of chain link fencing, each separated by a shared fence. For five dollars an hour you could get your swings in against a pitching machine that could be adjusted to throw fast balls and curves at speeds anywhere from sixty to ninety miles an hour. At the far end of each cage was a tarp, and, depending how hard the ball you hit impacted on the tarp, an electronic scoreboard (itself protected by a wire cage) would say "That drive went 400 feet, a homer to dead left in Fenway, but a warning track out in the Houston Astrodome and a lazy fly to center in Yankee Stadium."

I watched a few times wondering if I still had my swing. Seeing the ball come in at high speed took me back to my playing days and the night Dolph Hurley hit me. Most of the people hitting were young, some had pop in their bat, others didn't. Finally, one Friday afternoon, I broke down and bought an hour. I picked a bat from the rack near the front desk and rented a pair of batting gloves much like you would rent bowling shoes.

At first I was rusty, but thirty minutes in my swing came back and I was stinging the ball well. At one point I hit six consecutive shots out of Yankee Stadium in left and left center fields (I bat right handed.) Toward the end of my hour, I upped the speed of the machine to ninety miles an hour, all of them fastballs. I was still gun shy over facing a curve ball at any speed. The blind spot in my left eye hadn't gone away. It had gotten smaller over the years, and for practical purposes I could see to drive etc., but having a curve ball come at me, then disappear for a blink, was more than I could handle. I had a great time and began hitting the ball every Friday afternoon weather permitting.

It was during one of those Friday afternoons I met Ruthie Poncedeleone. She was in the batting cage next to me. She was tall and wiry. I noticed she left all of her weight on her back foot when she swung which reduced her power. She made contact but there was no pop in it. I didn't say anything figuring she might tell me it was none of my business. I was getting into my car when I saw her walking up on me. She introduced herself and asked me if I had ever played as she couldn't help but notice how well I hit the ball. I don't brag about playing professional ball, but it is a fact I am proud of even if it was the low minors.

"So, what do you think of my swing?" she asked.

"Well," I said "from the waist up it's not bad, but you're losing all your power down below."

She asked me to show her so I grabbed a bat from my trunk (I was bringing my own bat by now) and demonstrated how I swing and what she was doing.

We talked for a while, mostly baseball. She asked me if I would critique her throw as well. It turned out she played third base on a women's softball team made up of her and her fellow nurses. She was an LVN who worked at a nearby hospital. I agreed.

We met the next morning (Saturday) at 8 a.m. on one of several ball diamonds near the batting cages. I brought my glove. It was the same glove I used in the minors. It was smooth and worn and felt wonderful on my left hand. To a ballplayer, a glove is a tool, something that is regularly groomed and oiled.

We played catch for an hour. She had the same problem with her throw that she did with her swing. She was right handed and I got her comfortable with pushing off her back foot and completing the throw on her left leg. Her throws, like her swings in the batting cage, became increasingly stronger.

"You should come and see me play this afternoon," she said.

"Where and when?" I asked.

She pointed to a diamond several hundred feet across a parking lot in a complex of ball fields.

"Over there. At three o'clock."

So I went. My weekends were otherwise empty. I sat in wooden bleachers along third base. It was slow pitch. She took my advice in both her hitting and her throws from third to first. I must say she had a pretty good ball game. Afterwards she treated me to ice cream at a Dairy Queen. We agreed to see each other the following Friday and take batting practice together.

We started seeing each other, and not too much later began sleeping with each other. That was all pretty good. I made it clear to her early that I wasn't interested in marriage or living together. I liked her, and as long as we were both comfortable with our arrangement, we could keep it going. Then she used the "love" word.

She rolled over on a Saturday morning in bed and whispered it in my ear. It was the last thing I wanted to hear. I didn't respond, so she said "I love you" again only louder.

"I heard it," I said.

After that the weekend fell apart. She didn't say much of anything the rest of Saturday. Finally, we had it out on Sunday afternoon. I reminded her that I was honest up front about us.

"So you don't love me?" she asked. I didn't say anything. "You don't?" she asked. It ended with her curled up on the couch crying her eyes out. I heard her sobbing all the way out to my car.

I stayed away from her for three weeks. We didn't talk. I wasn't mad at her but the whole idea of being tied to one woman the rest of my life was second only to Dolph Hurley's fastball in the chops. I avoided the batting cages as well. I missed swinging the bat, but I missed Ruthie more. I finally broke down and called her.

"So you wised up," she said.

"I did," I admitted.

"Well, it's a good thing you called," she said, "because I was very close to moving on."

We started up where we left off. I realized she made a good difference in my life. I agreed to meet her family. My parents were both dead and my brother Freddie lived in Seattle so the family get together was a one-way affair. I went over to her parents' house for a Sunday lunch of roast beef and mashed potatoes. Ruthie got her Cajun name and dark looks from her father and her height from her German mother. She had four older brothers all of them pretty good high school athletes in various sports, baseball included. I hit it off well with the men in the family. They talked baseball with me most of the afternoon. I told them the jump from high school ball to pro baseball was huge. They were all nice guys and none had a chip on their shoulder. I've met ball players who didn't have what it takes to play anything more than high school ball and it became a pissing match with them shoving their macho in my face.

When the afternoon was over I thanked Mrs. Poncedeleone for the meal. A minute or so ahead of me, Ruthie left in her own car. As I sat in the front seat of my car, the window down, Mrs. Poncedeleone walked out of the house toward me.

"All my men play on their women," she said. "Even he does." She nodded toward her husband who could be seen sitting in the living room window. "I guess it's in their blood," she continued. "But hear this. You don't play on Ruthie. Ruthie gets her temper from me. You don't want me mad at you."

I made it clear to her my intentions with Ruthie were real. I proposed marriage to Ruthie several weeks later and we were married in the Catholic church. I have no religious affiliation but I married in Ruthie's church to make things go smoothly. We settled in.

We had two kids, a pair of fraternal twins, one a boy we named Felix and his sister, Felisha. I surprised myself at how I took to parenting. I was actually the better parent. Ruthie was dutiful but she didn't bond with her kids like you'd think a mother would. She continued to work the night shift at the hospital (she enjoyed working nights) so during the week I'd make the kids breakfast and get them ready for school. About the time Ruthie was coming in from work, I'd drive them to school. She'd give us all a peck on the cheek then she'd be off to bed. Later in the day she'd make the evening meal and have it warm for us, but by the time I got home, she was off to work again. I made it a point to alter my schedule so as to pick the kids up after school and be with them during the evening. It was me who went to the parent teacher meetings and the kids' extra curricular events.

Both our kids were exceptional athletes. Felisha took to softball much like her mother had. She and I began playing catch when she was barely six years old. By the time she was eight she had an arm better than most boys her age. I taught her fundamentals—how to keep her head down when she was picking up a groundball, how to square away to bunt and hit down on the ball when she needed to slap the ball by a charging third baseman.

Felix, on the other hand, took to dance. He had no interest in what you might expect a boy would go for. Football and baseball meant absolutely nothing to him. At age three, he enjoyed standing by the television and mimicking dancers on Soul Train and American Bandstand. I myself had no talent for dancing, and with Ruthie being mostly unavailable to both kids, Felix didn't get the attention or the encouragement Felisha got with her softball. But as Felix grew into his dancing, I never missed a recital or a school play. I attended every performance Felix was in, sat front row, and let him know I was there for him.

It wasn't too much after my kids turned fifteen that I figured them both for gay. It was becoming clear that Felisha liked girls more than boys and Felix liked boys more than girls. I could just sort of tell by the way they carried themselves. I was sitting on our patio in the back yard on a Sunday. Ruthie was at work. The kids were checking in with me before they left. Felicia had a softball game and Felix was off to the movies with a pair of school friends who were nice kids from nice parents but were definitely nonmainstream artistic types. Ruthie had developed no sense of fashion. Neither had I, but when it came to clothing, it was me who was left advising our children on how to dress.

"Felix," I said. He was wearing dark blue trousers with a dark blue turtleneck shirt resulting in no color contrast whatsoever. That, coupled with a brown belt, black loafers, and yellow socks, in my view, begged for my intervention.

"Yes, Dad."

"Son," I said "just a thought, but always make sure your belt and your shoes match. And it wouldn't hurt to have your shirt be a different color, or at least a different shade of color from your trousers. Make sure that if you wear dark trousers you wear dark socks as well. Something tells me you're destined for a world in which color coordination is going to be very important."

I looked at Felisha. She was in her baseball uniform. It was only a matter of time that she would look like her mother when I met Ruthie at the batting cage.

"Sweetie, you need to pull your socks up to your knees. They need to meet your pant legs at the knee. And tuck them under the cuff of your leggings. You want to look like a ballplayer. It's important." She dutifully took my advice. Felisha trusted every thing I told her about baseball.

Fifteen more years went by. I'd been married to Ruthie thirty-one years. I was fifty-nine years old. Ruthie was fifty-two. Felisha became a Houston police officer fresh out of high school. I was really proud of her. She was a patrolman for six years then became a homicide detective. She was tall and looked like her mother. Her partner was a slight woman, a doctor, who Ruthie and I took a liking to and accepted into our family circle.

Felix, however, didn't make it. He was murdered in New York walking home late at night from his job as a waiter. He moved there shortly after high school to pursue his dancing career. He had some minor success, landing work in a few small productions, but never anything approaching Broadway. After he left he didn't stay in touch with Ruthie and called me only two or three times a year. Our phone conversations were brief and shallow. We typically found out about him through his sister with whom he did maintain contact. He came home one Thanksgiving but was gone back in New York by Friday afternoon. I tried to be a good father to him. I honestly don't know what else I could have done. The man who murdered him was mentally ill. He hit Felix on the side of the head with a bottle as Felix was walking by.

I was sitting in a lawn chair on the patio on a summer evening gazing out at the back yard. The cicadas were humming away. The back yard had grown in beautifully. It was lush. I'd actually become interested over the years in gardening and had lost all interest in baseball. Go figure. I was happy in my job, good at it, so good in fact that it almost seemed too easy to make the money that was coming in. I missed Felix, but Felisha, thank goodness, was still close to Ruthie and me. I was happy our daughter was a detective and not exposed to the street violence a patrolman could face. Despite things turning out well for me I couldn't help but think I had already navigated much of life's river.

Ruthie pulled up a lawn chair next to me.

"Kenny," she said.

"Yeah," I said absently.

"I want a divorce."

That was Ruthie. She had been direct from the beginning. And it didn't surprise me that things were over. Our life was comfortable. She was still a nurse. The house was paid for. We had no problems. We rarely argued. I honestly think that Ruthie realized marriage was probably not for her but stuck it out all these years.

"Do you remember that time," I asked, "that you asked me if I loved you and you got upset because I didn't answer you?"

"I do," she said.

"Ask me again."

"So, Kenny, do you love me?"

"Yeah," I said. "But if it's over it's over."

And it was. Ruthie and I ended amicably. I told her she could have the house. She left me for a woman. A doctor! My two kids and my wife were gay and the two women in my life were lesbians who hooked up with doctors. I was the only heterosexual in the bunch.

I moved into an apartment in my old stomping grounds. I stayed close to Felisha and was still on good terms with Ruthie. The batting cages where I met Ruthie were long gone, replaced by a WalMart. My old little league was gone as well. The baby boomers had grown up and the neighborhood simply didn't have enough kids to maintain a league.

I had considered retirement but now my job was all I had. I was back to living the way I was when I met Ruthie. I missed my garden. I put several potted plants (roses, geraniums, daffodils) on the porch of my apartment. I wasn't in any hurry to meet women. It was just me, my job and my plants and that was fine.

As was my habit, I drove down I-45 on Wednesdays, making stops in several of the overlapping towns between Houston and Galveston. I normally made the drive between 8:30 and 9:00 to avoid as much of rush hour as possible. If things went smoothly, I made my last stop on the Wednesday route, in Galveston, at the Georgellen Club, around noon.

Through Luther, during the year he mentored me, I met George Jax, who was at the time the owner of the Georgellen Club. George liked and trusted Luther, and since Luther gave George his seal of approval on me, things started out well between George and me.

But two years in, after I had taken over for Luther, George Jax passed away. His heart blew out on him. The new owner, Tom York, took a while to warm up to me, but once he saw I was worthy of Luther's endorsement, and George Jax's trust, he and I formed a sound business relationship.

I made a brief visit into Tom's office. He expected me on Wednesdays. I took his order (beer, wine etc.) and we exchanged small talk for ten minutes or so. I said goodbye, then sat down in the restaurant portion of the club for a turkey sandwich, a house salad and one of the beers that pays my salary.

My favorite table in the club is in a corner with a wide view through an immense plate glass window of the Gulf of Mexico. From that table I have a view of ships moving along the horizon as they come and go. I sit and eat and drink thinking about the people on those ships as they go about their business, not realizing that someone is watching them. And who is watching over me? I guess I have an existential streak.

A young waiter who had taken my order came over with my bill. I paid him and tipped him well. Restaurant people work hard, and when they deliver good service, I reward them. He looked familiar. He was large, at least six feet three, with a long torso and arms to match. He couldn't have been over twenty.

"What's your last name?" I asked. The nametag he wore

on his shirt said *"Christian."*

"Christian Hurley" he said.

"Do you know Dolph Hurley?" I asked.

"He's my dad."

I pulled out a business card and gave it to young Christian Hurley.

"What does he do now?" I asked, "He pitched professionally, right?"

"He did. He sells cars now. Not far from here." He pointed down Seawall Boulevard to the west. "Five minutes from here."

I asked young Hurley to tell his dad Ken Burke said hello. I didn't know if anything would come of it, but I'm a sentimentalist, and if Hurley remembered me I figured we could reminisce. A month later I was back in the club, eating at the same table, watching the ships go by on the same horizon when Christian Hurley took my order.

"My dad would love to see you," he said. "In fact, he insisted."

I finished my meal, paid and tipped Christian, then took a short drive west to Island Motors. If I'd seen it once, I'd seen it one hundred times, but I never connected it with Dolph Hurley.

The lot was asphalt, with about twenty used cars parked neatly in three rows facing Seawall Boulevard. A small corrugated metal building sat at the back of the lot. I jumped out of my car and walked toward the building. A thin white man, clearly not Dolph Hurley, was talking to a well-built black man next to a black limousine. I knocked on the door of the small building. It opened, and there was Dolph Hurley, as I remembered him, but grey, wrinkled, and at least three hundred pounds. He shook my hand vigorously with the paw that ended my baseball career.

The office had a pair of soiled metal desks, each with its own chair, at opposite ends of the shack. Hurley sat behind a desk, and I pulled up a chair from the other. We had a friendly conversation. I'd lost touch with the game, but always knew Hurley had what it took to make it to the big leagues.

"I spent all or part of five seasons in the majors," he said.

"So, you didn't get a pension?" I asked.

"Nope," he said. "I didn't get there."

Hurley seemed like a different man, no longer brash, cocky. Once upon a time he came across as a bully. But Father Time can change a fellow. It had certainly changed me.

"I wanted to see you," he said. "When Christian told me you came into the Georgellen Club I hoped you'd stop by."

"This has been good," I said.

"But," he continued, "I really needed to square things with you."

We both knew there was an elephant in the room.

"I'm in A.A.," he said. "I'd like to apologize to you. I don't know how to fix things. If you ever need a job, you've got one here as long as I'm in business."

"I guess it's time," I said, "to ask why you hit me. I know you guys hated us and we hated you, but was it that bad?"

"No," said Hurley, "it wasn't the rivalry."

"What, then?" I asked.

Hurley and I, even back then, had no apparent bad blood between us.

"I thought you was queer," he said.

"Queer? You thought I was queer?"

"Yeah," he said.

I had told him, a few minutes earlier, I was divorced, with one child living and the other dead.

"Why'd you think that?" I asked.

"It was your socks. You wore your socks pulled all the way up to your knees. I figured a queer would wear his socks that way."

The Parole Officer

When I was eighteen I was raped by a man who picked me up while I was hitchhiking. My boyfriend at the time, a guy named Todd, and I had attended a July 4th party in Houston. Todd wanted to stick around an extra day with his friends, primarily to smoke dope and party. I, on the other hand, had promised my parents I would be home by the night of the 4th. So Todd and I had an argument that spelled the end of him and me. I should have called my parents to come and get me but that would have been an admission to them that Todd was the jerk they thought he was. Besides, it was 1968, the summer of love, and what could go wrong? Todd and I had thumbed rides most of the year we'd been going together, but I'd never tried it on my own.

The distance from southeast Houston (where we were partying) to Galveston (where I lived) was about forty miles. Todd didn't have a car. He was a year older than me and, but for bagging groceries on the island, had absolutely no direction. He wrote poetry and held himself aloof from the "system" so when I told him I was going home he tried to manipulate me by insinuating I was just another straight Catholic girl who was basically uptight, blah, blah, blah. One of the partiers, I recall his name as Rusty, volunteered to give me a lift home (a ride I should have taken) but I declined and walked onto the I-45 feeder road (heading south) and put out my thumb.

Interstate 45, then, as it is now, was a dangerous freeway. People, primarily young women, disappeared regularly along it. But when you're eighteen, you assume bad things don't happen to you. I wasn't out there fifteen minutes when I got a ride. The guy who picked me up wasn't bad looking. He had a surfer's look — tall, muscular, but lean with long brown hair turned yellow by the sun. We immediately started chatting, him telling me he was headed north on I-45 but turned back when he saw me, figuring he'd help me out. That gave me a bad vibe but I kept it to myself. It didn't take long for him to get down to business. He asked me if I smoked dope. I told him "no" (even though I did) and, ultimately, did I like to fuck around. Once again I told him "no". By then, I was scared. I didn't know what to do. I'm sure he could hear fear in my voice because I certainly could. Whereas, he'd been chatty initially, he got quiet. So did I, and with the windows down, the only sound in the car was the wind whipping through it.

It didn't surprise me at all when he pulled off the freeway onto the feeder road along an expanse of undeveloped coastal plain. In 1968 the myriad of small towns that speckled I-45 didn't overlap, so there was plenty of scrub and bush that went on for miles. I was in trouble.

He pulled into an abandoned gas station, its paint chipping, boarded, the pumps rusting. "I have syphilis," I lied. He said nothing. Instead, he drove around to the back of the gas station. There he pulled a knife from his boot (he was wearing a tee shirt and blue jeans) brandished it, and said "you can live through this, but only if you behave." So, in the back seat of his car (a blue Chevy Malibu) he raped me. It lasted all of a few minutes, but I anticipated my throat would be cut, my body dumped in the high vegetation behind the gas station. When it was over he pulled me out of the car, told me to face the open wasteland, and not turn around. He said if I didn't do as directed he would come back and kill me. I did what I was told, but I had a good look at him, I knew the make and color of his car, and I got the plates.

I sat down on the curb in front of the gas station for thirty minutes. It was dark. Cars roared by on I-45. I got up and started walking down the feeder road. I walked down to an intersection a mile or so away to a convenience store where I told the desk clerk what happened and could I borrow a quarter to make a call on the pay phone outside the store? He gave me the money. I made the call to my parents. He handed me a Pepsi Cola and let me sit on a stool he kept behind the counter. My parents arrived in twenty minutes, and I told them everything that happened.

The next morning my father called the Houston and Galveston police departments. At one point during breakfast my mother became hysterical. I'm an only child and it was becoming apparent to the three of us I was lucky to be alive. Both police departments listened, but the most helpful were the Island police. My gut feeling is that rather than fight over whose case it was, the Houston police let the Galveston people have it. I was a resident of Galveston, and I was headed in that direction when the rape occurred.

We went by John Sealy Hospital where I was pronounced OK. The ER, as I assume was its practice in such a case, took a vaginal specimen to preserve the rapist's semen assuming there was any. I was raped at about seven pm, and went to the hospital late the next morning, more than twelve hours later. My parents were inexperienced at this, as was I, so by the time my parents composed themselves, then reported the event to the police, all that time had gone by.

A black police officer, Nathan Livingston, interviewed me. My mother asked if it wouldn't be more appropriate for a female detective to interview me, but I made clear to my parents that it was me who got raped and detective Livingston, who had assured us that such crimes were his area of expertise, was fine by me. (Even in the state I was in, bewildered, angry, violated, there would be no truce in the battle for control of my life going on between my mother and me.)

I gave detective Livingston the make of the car, the plates and a description of the man who raped me, detailing everything from the minute he picked me up until he sped off.

"Here's the problem, Ms. Rusk," said Livingston. "If we do catch this guy, and not many rape victims give us as much detail as you have, you and I know it's his word against yours. In this culture, sorry to say, girls hitchhike, girls smoke dope along with their boy friends, and the sex going on out there is free and easy."

"So you don't believe me?" I asked.

"I believe you. I mean that. But when I take this to the Galveston County DA, the prosecutor working your case is going to kick it back at me. Did anybody at all see what happened? This report from John Sealy shows you weren't beaten or bruised in the rape. I have to prove this. You do understand that?"

I did, and we left. The ride home was sullen. Two days later I received a call from Nathan Livingston. My mother took the call, but I pulled the phone from her hand.

"Ms. Rusk," he said.

"Yes."

"Your rapist has confessed."

I leaned back into the chair I had settled in to.

"What happened?" I asked.

"He walked in and confessed."

"Why?" I asked.

"The truth be known," said Livingston, "his conscience got to him. He said he'd never done anything like that before. Apparently he was angry at a girl he had just broken up with. His parents were with him. They seem like decent people. This is rare, I admit it, but that's how it unfolded."

"So what happens now?" I asked.

"He'll be charged with the lesser crime of sexual assault. His record is otherwise spotless. That fact that he came in, with an attorney I might add, made for a deal with the DA. What he did to you was aggravated sexual assault. He raped you after brandishing the knife. His actual crime was far more serious than what the DA will charge him with. But this isn't bad. I had little hope of this outcome. I hope you get some satisfaction from this."

"Will he go to jail?" I asked.

"Definitely. It won't be a long stretch. Probably two to five years. He'll probably serve about a third of that."

I hung up the phone and relayed the conversation to my parents. My father, a real estate attorney, pushed me to consider a civil lawsuit against the fellow. Surprisingly, my mother agreed with me when I said I wanted to wash my hands of the whole thing.

"You know," I said, "I didn't even think to get the guy's name."

I had planned to go to a Catholic college in Houston come the fall but I wasn't ready for that. It hit me what had happened and I went into a depression that was marked by intermittent anxiety then sadness that kept me in my room for days at a time. I went through therapy. The road back would be a long one.

I stayed a recluse in my parents' home for almost a year. My parents and I eventually healed. (My mother made a special trip to Todd's grocery job where she dressed him down in front of a store full of shoppers.) Ultimately, I knew it was time to rejoin the world. I decided to keep things simple. I had no intention of going to college any time soon.

My mother had an old friend on the island who she had grown up with. The two were like sisters. They had gone through elementary and high school together and had been in each other's weddings. Mary (that was the friend's name) had a daughter, Loren, who was my age. Our mothers sort of assumed Loren and I would become best friends just as our parents had, but we never really clicked. Loren was nice, but she was more of a social animal than me, and I always saw her as someone set on running with the popular kids.

But I must say that Loren came through for me when it counted. She had worked as a waitress at the Georgellen Club, a local bar restaurant, our senior year in high school. She had been off to college in Austin her freshman year and returned to work for the summer. She called me, at the urging, I'm sure, of both our mothers, and asked me would I like to give waitressing a try. She promised nothing, but knew that the owner, George Jax, was staffing up for the busy summer. I was reluctant, both anxious and demure. I wanted to go to college someday, and feared that if I delayed any longer, I might never go. But I knew I wasn't quite ready for the type of focus college demanded. I wanted to stay close to home. So I took Loren up on her offer and received an interview with George Jax.

I'd seen Mr. Jax around town but had never connected him with the Georgellen Club. He was a short thick man who I noticed regularly strolling along the sea wall. The interview was a little scary. It shouldn't have been, but I'd been such a shut-in for eleven months that the world seemed out of kilter.

"I know a bit about your story," he said.

"Then you know I was raped?"

He nodded.

"I guess Loren told you?"

"She did. She told me you would probably be nervous."

"To be honest with you, Mr. Jax, I plan on going to college someday. I don't plan on doing this forever."

"I haven't offered you a job yet, much less a lifetime career."

The interview went fairly well. George Jax and I visited

for an hour. We talked about my prior work experience. It wasn't much. I babysat from the time I was in the eighth grade through my sophomore year in high school. The summer of my junior year in high school I worked for my dad shooting copies and running errands.

"Are you capable of working hard? I mean, really hard?" he asked.

"I think so," I responded.

"Because when this restaurant is full, and it is on the weekend, you'll be going non-stop for most of eight hours. Do you think you can hold up to that?"

"I'd like to try."

"I need summer help. This would be a great work experience for a young person. You'll learn what honest hard work is. You'll learn a trade you can always fall back on if times get tough. You'll learn about people. This is a people business. You'll learn about yourself. And this benefits me as well. I've got a well-trained group of students who come back here in the summer ready to work on an as needed basis. I'll hire you, but I need a commitment to be responsible and work hard. To be clear, Miss Rusk, going forward, I'm sympathetic about what happened to you, but if you take a job at the Georgellen Club, I won't treat you any differently than any other staff member."

I took the job. George Jax and I shook hands. He commented on my strong grip. (My dad taught me always to shake hands firmly.) He told me I would work from 2:00 p.m. until closing Friday, Saturday, and Sunday nights when the summer crowds were at their peak. He also informed me that Wednesday would be a swing day for me, working a relief shift on occasions. I went to work the next day, a Sunday.

Loren didn't train me. A lady named Sonya Samuels did. She had been a full time waitress at the Georgellen Club for ten years. I shadowed her for six shifts then was turned loose on my own. Sonya changed my view of waitressing. I'd thought it would be a simple matter of walking up on a table, taking the order, and then bringing the meal to the table. But the Georgellen Club was a top notch place. Sonya taught me how to present the customer with a tour of the menu. I not only had to be a student of the menu, but I had to know and explain the specials of the day as well as the wine list. The job required thought, energy, and personality.

The summer went by fast. Loren went back to college. She gave me a warm hug. I was wrong about her. She had far more depth than I gave her credit for. Fall came and went. I liked the work. Tips were good. I saved money. George Jax gave me a raise. I did some serious thinking about what I wanted to do. The rape convinced me the world was made up of good guys and bad guys. There was no gray for me.

I learned that the name of the guy who raped me was Jeff Miller. My father found out. At first I became anxious, but I felt some relief knowing my rapist had gone to prison, even if it was a light sentence due to his coming forth and his clean record.

I decided to pursue a career in criminal justice. Come the spring semester, I enrolled at the island junior college. I took it slow. I hadn't been in school for over a year and a half. Studying was tough at first but, with a purpose in life, I devoured it.

While in school I kept my job at the Georgellen Club. I balanced work and school, which was tiring at times, but the rape motivated me. I stayed focused and became an "A" student.

Two years later I finished my courses at the Island community college. I wanted a four-year degree just in case law school was in my future. I decided it would be best for me to finish college away from Texas. I was twenty-two years old, living at home, and had no real world experience. I needed that in order to grow up. I applied to and was accepted at several schools that offered my degree. I chose a school in Kearney, Nebraska. The staff was friendly and responded to me.

I said goodbye to the Georgellen Club. George Jax made

it clear I would have a job if I ever needed one. I was sad, a little scared, but I was ready to move on. College life was successful. Being twenty-two was an advantage. And if any good came from the rape, it was that it matured me. Very little upset me. I was an excellent student on a mission.

I met Naomi Marks, a girl from Emporia, Kansas. Naomi was a strawberry blonde who blushed quite a bit. She grew up on a farm and was an incoming freshman, while I, though a junior in rank, was new to the school and to the heartland. She and I met one day over lunch in the student center. I was sitting alone, early in the fall semester, pouring over a psychology book, when she walked up, tray in hand, asking could she sit with me. I wasn't lonely, and frankly, since the rape, had become somewhat solitary. But Naomi had an irresistible personality. She was an open book. We hit it off well and became close friends, studying together, eating in the cafeteria regularly, and watching old movies in our dorm rooms.

Naomi was engaged to Frank Mercer. Frank was my age and had finished college with a degree in agricultural finance. He had recently taken the job as ranch manager on Naomi's family ranch, which, I came to learn, was a huge cattle operation outside of Emporia. Frank visited Naomi at least one weekend per month. And Naomi reciprocated with visits back to Emporia with similar frequency. I couldn't tell if they were in love or not. Whereas Naomi was very physical and affectionate, Frank was a bit more reserved fitting the stereotype of the mid-western male.

When I was around, there always seemed to be a bit of tension coming from Frank during his visits. I went, at the invitation of Naomi, to dinner and a movie a few of the times Frank came to visit. But my better sense had me bow out of such overtures from Naomi when Frank visited as I felt that their times together were personal and did not need a third party tagging along. It also made me feel a bit foolish as well.

Naomi and I grew close over the next two years and I

believe Frank came to resent it. He never stated his insecurity directly to Naomi, nor to me, but I could sense it. About a year into our friendship, while sitting with Naomi on a bench, talking about whatever, I hugged her and planted a firm kiss on her cheek. And to be honest, I was attracted to Naomi. I'd had it with men. My experience with Todd, then the fellow who raped me, left me completely distrustful of that gender. Naomi blushed, picked up her books and rushed away.

For the better part of a month it was quite uncomfortable between us. We nodded, stopped occasionally to make small talk, but there was a cool reserve now evident in Naomi that was usually apparent in Frank. I don't know if she mentioned the kiss to Frank or not.

Finally, she came around. We had a serious talk. She asked me what the meaning of the kiss was as she had interpreted it in a sexual sense. I told her that since my rape my sexual preference had become confused, that I was indeed physically attracted to her, but our friendship meant so very much to me. Could she, I asked, find it in her to get past our awkward moment?

To no surprise, Naomi was quite forgiving. She made it clear she was past the event. We took up where we had left off as boon companions.

A year later I graduated, with honors, my degree in criminal justice. My parents were there. My mother cried. My dad asked me could he use his legal influence to connect me with a job opportunity? In that, I was not interested. I was determined to do things on my own. Naomi and Frank attended as well. Frank shook my hand warmly and gave me a perfunctory hug.

I interviewed in several states, but took a job as a parole officer in Harris County, Texas. I was excited to begin my career. I had quite a few cases thrown on me from the onset so you could say that I hit the ground running. I was mentored along the way by experienced parole officers who took me under their wings. I think it's fair to say that I treated my parolees fairly. I wasn't looking to send them back to prison, but I made it clear to each of them I would tolerate no nonsense. One fellow stated to me that he was connected to high-level drug people and that if I sent him back, he could have me killed. I recommended that he be sent back to resume his sentence and he was. At the hearing he stared at me but the tactic didn't work.

As coincidence would have it, I was assigned the case of Trina Ball, the niece of Sonya Samuels who trained me years before at the Georgellen Club. Sonya, Trina informed me, had died of a stroke two years before. I should have recused myself from the case but decided that I owed Sonya a solid. Trina was paroled from the womans' facility in Lockhart, Texas. She was doing a twenty sentence for possession of a controlled substance with intent to distribute. Like most women in prison, there was a man on the other end of her life. In her case, she and her boyfriend at the time were caught at the Texas-Mexico border near Laredo smuggling a large quantity of marijuana into the United States. I went easy on her, but during her parole she went right back to her tired ways of drug use and muling for the dealers. I had her sent back to prison despite her playing the "Sonya" card on me one last time.

I turned into a good parole officer if I do say so myself. The man who raped me, Jeff Miller, served his time and faded away. A few years after I took the job for Harris County, Naomi and Frank got married. I was a bridesmaid and truthfully felt a little funny dressed up in a gown and wearing make up. My normal attire was a business suit or, on the weekends, blue jeans and a tee shirt or blouse.

I wanted to get some time alone with Naomi, to catch up on things, but she was busy the whole time. A dinner and a dance followed in the hall of the nondenominational church where the wedding took place. A fellow named Rob asked me to dance several times during the evening. I'm a clumsy dancer. Actually, even thinking of myself as any kind of dancer is an exaggeration. I danced with Rob and visited with him most of an hour. He was a nice fellow, handsome, but at the end of the evening, when Naomi and Frank left for their honeymoon, it occurred to me that I had not a scintilla of interest in men.

Naomi and I stayed in touch. She and Frank had two children, a son (Gunther) and his younger sister, (Judith.) I was Judith's godmother. Over a ten-year period I made several trips to Emporia—three Thanksgivings and a week in the summer, and developed a warm relationship with both children. Frank was always courteous to me, but he never fully trusted me to be alone with Naomi. Wherever Naomi and I were together, Frank was there too.

My career as a parole officer went exceptionally well. I climbed the ranks, received sterling reviews. Eventually I managed a section of parole officers from whom I expected nothing short of excellence. My mother passed away when I was fifty, and a few years later my father went in to assisted living at a nice clean place on the Island. Because I lived in Houston, it was easy for me to drop in on him regularly.

The Georgellen Club was now owned by Tom York. George Jax had passed away. My visits to the Georgellen Club became less frequent. On rare occasions, after visiting my dad, I might stop in at the club and have a meal. I especially liked sitting in my old section, watching young waiters and waitresses do what I did years before, wondering if they were as uncertain of the future as I was. Every now and then I would receive a card from Loren, but I hadn't seen her in at least thirty years.

One afternoon, while I sat in the club nursing a margarita, my old boyfriend Todd walked up on me. I saw him approaching, and, despite being heavier and thinning on top, he was the same fellow I thought I had a future with many years ago. I was cordial, but not engaging. We exchanged a few pleasantries. He had become a high school teacher, was divorced with three children, and was recently retired. Could he, he inquired, buy me dinner some time? I gave him a definite "no," wished him an obligatory "good luck," and watched him stroll away.

Two years later I received a phone call from Frank informing me that Naomi had died. She had fallen in the bathroom and bashed her head on the tile floor. (Even in college, Naomi sleepwalked on occasions.) Needless to say, I was shocked. I jumped on a plane, rented a car and drove to the same church that Naomi and Frank had been married in. It was an eloquent service. The minister, a large man with a strong booming voice, did justice to the life of Naomi Marks. Gunther and Judith were grown. I knew that we would see little or nothing of each other as they formed their own families and got on with their lives. Frank was still Frank. He shook my hand, and thanked me for coming.

In the parking lot, as I stood by my rental car, the door opened to allow some fresh air inside, the minister who delivered the eulogy approached me. Standing at a far end of the parking lot, under a tree, were a woman and a teenage boy. He came closer and I studied his eyes, a talent of mine that had come in handy in my years of law enforcement.

"Does your flock know it has a confessed rapist preaching to them on Sundays?"

"That they do," he said.

"You know," I said, "I almost got out of here without recognizing you. But your voice hasn't changed all that much and your eyes haven't either. You've put on quite a bit of weight, however."

"You have a good memory," he said.

"How could I not?" I asked.

I looked toward the woman and the boy standing under the tree.

"Do they know what you did?"

"They do."

"What do they think about it?"

"They know me as the man I am now, as do my parishioners."

I studied this fellow, this rapist, this man who changed my life. I had wondered, over the years, what I would do, what I would say, if we ever met. I was speechless.

"Might I have your forgiveness?" he asked.

"Come again?"

"Might I have your forgiveness?"

"Yes," I said, "if you can tell me my name."

He stood silently, his head down, I assume embarrassed.

"You don't even know my name, do you?"

After a pregnant silence he said, "I do not."

I let him walk away unforgiven. He would get no relief from me.

I got into my car, drove to the airport, where I caught my plane. When I was eighteen my life took an unforeseen turn. Was I better for it? I couldn't say.

The Power Broker

I didn't always love power. It just sort of grew on me. Allow me to explain how such a thing can happen.

So there I was, a forty-one year old CPA with a girlfriend, Mildred, whose parents, Bob and Candy Embry, thought me unworthy of their daughter. It was 1992. I had spent the evening at the home of the Embry's in Galveston, Texas where I enjoyed a nice supper of roast, potatoes, and apple pie. It was at that dinner that I decided Mildred was not the girl for me. I couldn't stand her mother, and I didn't love Mildred enough to endure three or more decades of Candy's chronic nit picking. Bob was a nice enough guy. We'd gone to a few Rice (his alma mater) football games together, but he was henpecked and I had simply seen too many similarities between mother and daughter (an only child.) That night at dinner, as Mildred's foot tapped mine under the table, a reminder that I was using the wrong fork for my apple pie, something clicked in my bean counter mind that said, "Adam, don't do this."

Rather than riding out the evening in front of a roaring fire, I excused myself early, using the pretense that my drive back to Houston on what promised to be an inclement evening, merited my departure. I shook Bob's hand, gave Candy and Mildred each a peck on the cheek, and promised to call Mildred upon my safe arrival at my Houston apartment. I dreaded hurting

Mildred. She was a sweet girl but I could see her turning into her mother. Good fellow that he was, Bob Embry was not someone I would allow myself to become. I felt a sense of deep relief, something I had not experienced in months, as I pulled away from the Embry's driveway in my Toyota Corolla.

And that is where luck intervened. (Bear in mind that at this stage of my life I distinguish between luck and opportunity. Luck, as I define it now, is unwarranted good fortune that jumps into your lap. Opportunity, on the other hand, requires an act of seizure, by the opportunist, before it can beget success. Linguists, philosophers, and scholars may beg to differ, but I am currently sitting on ten billion dollars, give or take.)

But on that night twenty-three years ago on my way out of town, I was contemplating no such distinction. I stopped into a mom and pop grocery for a candy bar, something I didn't need (I was overweight and full of Embry meat, potatoes and pie.) But I was going to celebrate, by God, and sugar was how I was going to do it.

I walked into the store, bought my candy bar and walked out. Ahead of me as I left the store, was a drunk. He swayed like a drunk. He smelled like a drunk. He carried in his left hand a six-pack of what drunks drink. He was dressed professionally, in a white shirt with dark pants, his tie loosened at the collar. He had at least ten years on me and for an instant I wondered if he was lonely. Had he at one time broken things off with his "Mildred" only to find himself drinking alone in the blue glow of his television on a Friday night such as this?

His car was parked next to mine, and with overburdened hands, he fumbled with his keys allowing a small piece of paper to fall to the asphalt below and be carried by a chill north wind to my feet as I stood at the front of the store. Out of courtesy I picked it up. It was a lottery ticket.

The lottery, though it seductively offered instant wealth, held no attraction for me. What disposable income I had went to the stock market, a pedantic exercise that, with time, I was confident would pay off. I waived the ticket at the fellow as he sat in his car turning on its ignition. He looked at me and offered no expression other than the dull blank stare of the disengaged. He drove off leaving me with an item I neither wanted nor cared about. But now, I supposed, I owned it and, rather than giving it back to the store, placed it in my back pocket without so much as reading its numbers. I arrived home, phoned Mildred, and fell soundly to sleep.

The next morning I arose and showered wondering how I might tell Mildred of my decision to let her go. I concluded that I would be direct, face-to-face, with calcium in my spine. I called her and arranged for lunch at our favorite restaurant in Galveston the following day, Sunday, at noon. With that I said goodbye and took my several shirts and the trousers I had worn the night before to a local cleaners. On a whim, I pulled the lottery ticket from the trousers and setting it on my dresser.

Lunch was the ordeal I expected, a mix of happiness and chatter on the part of Mildred, quiet resolution by me. I paid the bill and, in the parking lot, broke her heart. I drove away, Mildred sobbing and screaming, "What did I do? What did I do?" It troubled me a bit that leaving her didn't trouble me more.

I spent the remainder of Sunday afternoon reading the newspaper. The phone rang several times. I didn't pick it up. And then I saw the numbers. I hadn't given the lottery ticket a second thought but when I noticed on the City page the winning sequence of 5-11-23-29-42-50, I went to my room and checked.

So what is it like winning $30 million dollars? Better stated, what is it like having $30 million dollars find you? Not as exciting as one might think. Stupefying more aptly describes it. I didn't believe it at first. I sat in my chair, the newspaper tossed on the floor, staring at the wall. Thirty million dollars. If it were true, work, as I knew it, had come to an end. It certainly brought with it the need for planning and for discretion. I wasn't going to run out the door on a spending spree. I had to think. I *made* myself think.

I hid the ticket in a book for the evening, but wisely tucked it away in my safety deposit box bright and early the next morning. I had, to that point in my life, never really taken the time to define who I was. And it was essential here that I do that because the next sixty or more years were probably, absent the unforeseen, exclusively mine. Who was I? Who did I want to be?

The journey of self-discovery could wait. I made a phone call to the lottery commission and verified that no one had claimed the winning ticket. I made an appointment with a large established investment firm, well staffed with its battery of attorneys and financial advisors, who guided me in the creation of various and sundry trusts and other financial tools. I then approached the lottery commission and claimed my money. It was one month after that eventful night in front of the grocery store. Once my new winnings were funded, I gave two weeks notice at work citing a business opportunity as my reason for leaving. Thus began my new life.

But I was still in the larval stage, trapped in the cocoon of old thinking. I grew bored rather quickly. I'm not one who does well with idle time. I wanted something else. I was somewhat fascinated with the concept of acquisition, the exercise of control by man over nature, by men over other men. It wasn't long before I was buying up real estate. I saw where the city was going and I bought up large tracts of rural land not yet touched by the sprawling hand of Houston. I incorporated, remained silent in my control of the company, and lusted often after Houston. If I could have bought all of Houston I would have. When I left Mildred I felt nothing. When I won the very lottery that some men pray for, I felt neither joy nor excitement, but the sense of disbelief that comes with unexpected overwhelming change. Yet, when it came to land, more and more land, I felt a hunger I simply could not control.

And then I purchased my first human. He was an older fellow, up for reelection to the city council in another city, a large one. I contributed to his campaign. That experiment went rather well. I poured money into elections all over the Gulf Coast. I owned people on planning commissions, city councils and the legislature. I no longer estimated where cities would grow, I *decided* where cities would grow. I extended my tentacles to most of the state. I owned land, I owned buildings, I owned people, money cascaded, and some poor bastard, who, if he hadn't drank himself to death by now, had no idea that, but for a hand full of car keys, he could have been me.

At age forty-five I was worth my first billion dollars. I was alone in life, but really didn't care. People in high places knew me — politicians, fellow power brokers and the like. But I lived discreetly, moving like a shark in the shallows, being one of those people behind the people who make the decisions. I dined out one night, my bodyguard seated unobtrusively at a nearby table, when I saw Mildred. Her hair was shorter, but it was Mildred. I hadn't seen her since that day when I left her broken in a parking lot. She was with a fellow and, judging by their apparent rapport, she seemed happy. I could only assume that man with her was her husband. She caught me looking at her, her eyes appeared to scroll wondering perhaps who I might be. Then I was up and gone, my body guard strolling behind.

I decided I should probably marry. For love? No. For succession. For the transfer of power. I wanted a son. I believed in only the temporal so it would be my lineage that remained after me. I married a woman eighteen years my younger. And she produced. She gave me a male, but he was not the male I wanted. I gave her and the boy a good life. Needless to say, they wanted for nothing. But it became apparent that the boy was weak, not a leader but a follower. I tried. I took the boy under my wing. I groomed him to be, someday, a governor, or a senator, or who knew, perhaps the most powerful man in the world.

I eventually divorced. My wife had given me all that she could give. I gave her the financial security for a more than comfortable life. My son, the beneficiary of his own trust, gravitated toward his mother. That did not surprise me. Nor did it surprise me that neither mother nor son had anything to do with me. I didn't give his mother another thought, but he was my son. In the following years that I neglected him, he became a bum. He philandered. He engaged in frequent bacchanalia. How could I get from him what I wanted? I approached him with the following offer: "Give me an acceptable grandson, one that I can raise as my own son."

"Or what, Father? You'll take away my trust money?"

"That is exactly what I will do," I said.

And I would have and he knew it. So that boy, my son, my project, my protégé, the one within whom I had attempted to instill those things required to rule, one night took his life. I did not see that coming. He left a note and in it said that he had never been happy, because he could never make me happy. But I had not trained him to be happy. I trained him to be powerful. And the way he did it, the way he killed himself—he stole my car and crashed it into a tree. My car! My Mercedes!

I had felt very few things in my life, but I did feel the death of my son. I adjusted. The boy was simply not cut out to be the man I had projected. I had my chauffeur drive me around Houston, distracting myself with the buildings I owned.

I was sixty-five and worth ten billion dollars. One afternoon I took a drive on my own to Galveston. My bodyguard advised against it, my chauffeur was puzzled by it. I just wanted to get out and drive.

I stopped in at the Georgellen Club. I frequented the club during my CPA days but had been in it only a few times during the last ten years. I sat across the street from what used to be the small grocery that was the epicenter of my wealth. I purchased the grocery several years ago and built upon it a parking garage. The land increased yearly in value and the garage provided a steady stream of income. It was a cash register sitting atop a small gold mine.

I wanted the Georgellen Club as well. I envisioned it a four star hotel with a splendid view of the Gulf of Mexico. George Jax, its previous owner, now deceased, had refused to sell it to me as did the current proprietor, Tom York. Embedded, apparently, within the personal code of each man was a sense of loyalty. For Jax, it was the memory of his wife. For York, it was Jax.

I sat on the deck of the club, sipping iced tea, choosing to watch, rather than the placid Gulf, cars come and go from the parking garage. It was midday in midweek, so the club was not busy. Seated not far from me, drinking coffee and musing over some sort of report, was a middle-aged woman. I am neither prone to approaching people nor giving out my name yet this moment would be an exception.

"My name is Adam Allen," I said as I stood at her table. "I am not here to pester you. Trust me, I don't need to. But you look very familiar to me."

The woman looked up from her report.

"I don't know you," she said. "Tell me your name again."

"Adam Allen."

I sensed the wheels turning in her head as she rifled through names.

"My mother knew you," she said.

"Your mother is Mildred Embry," I remarked.

"Mildred Embry Evans," she corrected.

"And how is she?" I asked.

"She's gone," said the woman.

"I am sorry to hear that," I said.

"My father was Kyle Evans. He's dead as well," she said.

"I didn't know him," I said.

49

We visited for fifteen minutes. She was a school teacher who had at one time waitressed at the Georgellen Club.

"Your name," she said, "came up a few times. I sensed there was something between you and mother at one time."

"We were close once," I said. "Life was good to her, I hope."

"Mother had a satisfying life. She had few, if any, regrets."

I shook her hand and took my leave. I stopped on my way out of town in the parking lot of the restaurant where I had left Mildred standing more than twenty years before. As I drove back to Houston I wondered if I would have been a different man had I married her. I doubted it. I was who I was. I realized for a brief instant that I had allowed myself to become sentimental.

The Irish Man

My father made bombs for the IRA. I didn't know him well. What little I did learn of him came reluctantly from my mother. He was not typical Irish. He didn't drink and he had no poetry in him. His name was James "Jimmy" Tierney and he hated Protestants. In that regard, I suppose the acorn didn't fall far from the tree.

He came to America from Northern Ireland in 1939, a twenty-one year old mechanical engineer who settled in Baltimore where he worked in the ship building industry. There he met my mother, Rose Brown, at a picnic given by Saint Patrick Catholic Church. And then they had me.

My father stayed in America three years. Why he wanted to go back to Ireland is unclear to me. He broke the news to Mother that we, as a family, were moving to Belfast. My mother initially balked at going with him but eventually gave in. I assume he had, by the time we left, enough of America. Or perhaps it was his own father, a man I met but once, who persuaded him he was needed at home.

In Belfast, he went to work for a small engineering firm. He was always somewhat of a mysterious figure for me, coming in late at night, working six or more days a week, spending a perfunctory Sunday afternoon with me and Mother.

In Belfast, I learned to hate Protestants. It was easy. I joined a Catholic gang at thirteen, dedicated to vandalizing Protestant shops and churches. My father offered no resistance. I heard my parents argue over my waywardness. My mother wanted that hate to play no such role in my life. She threatened to divorce my father and take me back to America.

Then a bomb went off in downtown Belfast. Shards of glass maimed and killed people. It was big, all over the news. The police came to our home. Our doors were kicked in. My father was arrested. He went to prison for life. It was the opening my mother needed.

She moved us to Houston Texas—hot, humid, and initially unbearable. Her cousin Mary lived there. We started anew. Mother took a secretarial job. She placed me in Catholic high school. I was a United States citizen, born here, but with no real attachment to what seemed like a foreign country to me.

I was miserable in high school. I didn't study. I made no friends. I became reclusive and unruly. I began fighting. I was rough, having roamed Belfast streets. The Jesuits expelled me. Mother sent me to public school. That was worse. I schooled with coloreds, with Mexicans and worst of all, Protestants.

I left school at eighteen. It was 1957. I was clever, but virtually uneducated. America was prospering. World War II and Korea were behind us. I found work in a tavern. I bartended. I met women. I drank. I learned the business.

I turned thirty. It was 1970 when my mother died. She collapsed at work. She was fifty-one. I was living at home. She and I shared an apartment. I was leaving for work when I took the call. I wrote my father in prison of Mother's death. I heard nothing from him. A few work friends and I attended the funeral. Mother's cousin Mary had moved to Kansas City, but she flew in to attend. Beyond my imprisoned father and distant cousin, I had no one. Mother was my family. For several days I considered my treatment of her. I held myself accountable for her troubled and damaged heart.

A lawyer contacted me. His name was Townes. He held a letter from my mother. It directed him to contact me about a life insurance policy. We talked. I went to Mother's safe deposit box. I produced the policy. Lawyer Townes contacted the underwriter. I received a check in the mail for one hundred thousand dollars. I had money. I paid Mr. Townes for his work. I took stock of my life. I committed myself to frugality and responsibility. I was attentive to opportunity.

Dave Coogan came along. I liked him. He was Irish. He was Catholic. He was my kind of people. He was a CPA. We partnered in the purchase of a bar. I brought money to the table. He brought business acumen. He appeared stable. He had a young wife. He had two beautiful young girls. We prospered temporarily. And then the gambling began.

He came to me. It was late. The bar was closed. I was washing glasses. I was doing what responsible entrepreneurs do. He was disheveled. He was ashen. He had been drinking. He was shaking.

" Liam," he said, " I am in terrible trouble."

He owed the wrong people money. A large sum of money. Big green money. Could I help him? Could I save him? He confessed. He bared his soul. He had falsified our books. He had skimmed our money. He said he was a sick man. He said gambling owned his soul. He had until tomorrow evening to produce the money. "For the love of God, Liam, please help me."

I told him I would consider it. I went home. I thought about it. I slept feverishly on it. I called Mr. Townes. He drafted an agreement. He produced it in fast time. I would pay Dave Coogan's gambling debt in exchange for his portion of our business.

I called Dave Coogan. We met at our bar. I explained the terms. He had no choice. He took the deal. He signed the agreement in front of a notary. After closing two fellows showed up. They were large. They were serious. They said little. I produced cash. I handed them five stacks of big green money.

I said, "How do I know this matter is settled?"

One laughed. He said, "In this business there are no receipts." They left.

Dave Coogan begged me to take him back. He swore he was done gambling. He had a young wife. He had two young girls. He had another on the way. What would he do? I told him to leave. I told him we were through. I told him he had breached my trust. Trust was all I had with people. I heard several years later he was dead. Details were sketchy. A woman not his wife killed him. She had a gun. He had it coming.

So there I was. I had my own place. I was solo. I was blessed. I was ecstatic. I had unfettered access to the American dream. I was provident. I saw Houston growing. I saw Houston metastasizing. I relocated. I reinvented. I renamed my bar. I christened her Woodley's. Don't ask me why. I saw it in my dream. And in that dream were people, an ocean of the young and the promiscuous spreading south and west into strip malls and apartments that sprung up overnight—young professionals, blue collared construction workers oozing testosterone, secretaries, nurses, all of them bringing me big green money.

I fell in love. I violated a personal tenet. I would never marry I promised myself. I would play with the Mollys and Pollys and Dollys of the world but I would promise them nothing beyond short-term fun. Then Colleen Baker entered my life. Change my fundamental view of marriage she did not. She forced no such institution upon me. But I was happy, unwittingly happy and asked for her hand. She accepted. We had a son, Flynn. We were good for a while. We had our problems but the slope of our marriage never arced downward. We went stale temporarily. She had an affair. I suspected her of cheating. I had her followed. Her infidelity was corroborated. We talked. We got through it. We did it for us. We did it for Flynn.

Colleen had the bad habit of talking, the nonstop variety. She talked at breakfast. She talked at lunch. She talked at dinner. It's a wonder Flynn became a quiet boy. She talked behind the wheel of her car. She ran a red light. Colleen talks no more.

Flynn and I made a go of it. He was fourteen. I was forty-nine. I was tempted to remarry for the sake of the boy, but time went by as it does. I raised Flynn well, a strict and dogmatic Catholic. We attended mass without fail. We received the sacraments. I sent him to the finest Catholic high school Houston could offer. I sent him to Notre Dame. And then he betrayed me. His graduation within reach, he brought home a Protestant. A Lutheran! They were engaged. I protested. I commanded him, in her very presence, not to marry that girl. But he did. He went over me. So I disowned him. He was no longer my son. He was dead to me. I have no idea where he and his Protestant are or what they are doing.

I met George Jax, a man of my own ilk. It was at first uncomfortable. He was competition. He owned several bars. I owned just one. He offered to buy me out. I refused. He offered to partner with me on a pro rata basis, him the controlling partner. I refused. He hired Tommy York away from me, assuming I couldn't recover from such a loss, but I did. He finally gave up his aspiration to own my bar.

We became friends. Both of us proud and stubborn, we eventually recognized ourselves in each other. George had a wonderful wife, Ellen. He had a young daughter, Julia. They had me to dinner. We went fishing on their boat regularly in the Gulf of Mexico. They treated me like I was family, an uncle to their child.

And then Ellen passed away leaving George, much like me, a widower with a child. Leukemia got Ellen. Here today, gone tomorrow. George was neither Catholic nor Protestant, but a nonbeliever. Had he been a Protestant I could have gotten past it, so good a fellow he was. The Lord should have taken George before Ellen, or certainly along with her, for when she died George was dead too. He walked among the living, but that was as far as it went. I offered to watch over Julia should anything happen to him, but George assured me that Tommy York had filled that void. Then George passed away. He died strolling on the beach. I attended both his and Ellen's funerals. I have yet to weep in this life, but at those two funerals, I came very close. Other than Mother, no one has been as generous or accepting of me as George and Ellen Jax. I miss them dearly.

Father Time came a knocking. I got old. I turned seventy. It happened in the blink of an eye. One minute I was a kid, making life miserable for Protestants in Belfast, the next, there I was, looking in a mirror at a saggy face and a sack of flesh housing old bones and creaking joints. More over, I had lost my passion for success. I reworked my will, leaving every bit of a pretty penny to the Catholic Church. I asked Tommy York, now the owner of the Georgellen Club, would he be interested in buying Woodleys? But he was not. I sold everything, lock, stock and barrel, but for my house in Houston, and retired. I regretted it. I grew bored. I walked, I read, I kept up with politics. I continually wrote the archbishop, and ultimately, the Pope, about the unacceptable creep of liberalism invading Holy Mother the Church.

At least once a month I jump into my car for a drive to Galveston where I lunch with Tommy York. He is a grand fellow. He treats me well. He takes a good hour or so to sit and visit with me over my meal. He has offered me a job as a bartender, an old skill of mine, and I may take him up on that.

I received a letter from, of all people, my father in Belfast. He turned ninety-two and was released from his prison. He asked could he come and live with me? He was penniless. He had no one other than me. He had nowhere to go. I answered him in written form: *May you spend your last days by the sea and may the earth continue to melt.*

The Farm Boy

I was raised on a farm in Luke, Texas but I didn't want to be a farmer. I had other plans. Then death and love and heartbreak came along and changed things.

I played six man football for Luke High School and, if I do say so myself, was good. My goal was to play college football then become a coach at the highest level. I set my sights on the NFL and why not? Some of the great coaches of all time had humble beginnings. My path would be as follows: I would walk on, without an athletic scholarship, to any junior college football program that would take me. There were several in the area, and, since junior college ball in Texas was second to none, I felt I could land at any one of many throughout the state and still pursue my dream. I was certain I could earn, after playing (and excelling) at that level, if not a scholarship to one of the SWC schools, a free ride to a small school in Division-II or the NAIA. After that, I would begin my coaching career in the high school ranks, then make my way through college coaching into the big time.

You may ask yourself, why, if he was so good, would he have to start his journey as a mere walk on to a junior college?

Why not the University of Texas? Or Texas A&M? Well, I was small. You wouldn't know it now because I have since filled out. But at the time I was six feet tall and weighed a strapping one hundred and forty pounds. I was, however, very strong. Farm work will do that. Driving a tractor, branding cattle, cutting brush, no matter how much your mother cooks for you, it is very tough to keep on weight. Combine that with football (I played basketball, baseball, and ran track as well) and I was constantly burning calories.

Then there was the stigma of six-man football. Despite the serious attitude taken toward high school football in Texas, six-man football was looked down upon. For one thing, the scores were off the chart. It was regular to see both teams combine for one hundred to one hundred fifty points in a single game. I can remember beating teams by the score of seventy-one to sixty-nine or eighty to seventy-four. It's a bit like a basketball game played by football players with an occasional tackle thrown in.

But the athletes, such as myself, were for real. And the speed of the game was entertaining. My cousin, Lon, in a game my senior year, videotaped the ninety-nine yard run I made late in the game to defeat our rival, Irby High School. Irby had us trapped on our one yard line when I took the ball and squeezed through an opening only a skinny kid like me could fit into. The race was on. I ran ninety-nine yards with six Irby Buffalos and five Luke Broncos within two or three yards of me the whole way. I could hear them breathing and cussing each other. On film it was hilarious.

We were coached well in the fundamentals. We learned to block and tackle. And playing six-man forced me to learn multiple positions. I played quarterback, halfback and receiver. I had, and still have, exceptional hand-eye coordination. I punted, kicked off and place kicked. I kicked a forty yard field goal to win a game. I am quite proud of that. It was a pressure kick.

I also played center. In one game, our regular center, Lloyd Listy, had diarrhea. Our quarterback, Wade Grimes, refused to take the snap under center, and because we, for some reason, had not mastered the shotgun formation, I switched positions with Lloyd for that game, me playing center and Lloyd playing halfback. Late in the game, us trailing by six points, Lloyd broke loose on what appeared to be a game-winning run. But after clearing the line of scrimmage, running alone, he took a knee at midfield fearing he would shit his pants. He still lives that one down.

I needed advice about what I wanted to do with my life. I knew my parents would be hurt by me wanting to leave the farm, and I wanted to talk to someone who had taken a similar path in life, so I went to my coach, Bobby Carl Tripp. Coach Tripp was a straight shooter who had played high school football in Texas, but rather than playing at the college level, had gotten a degree from Southwest Texas State in education and combined it with a coaching career that started at Luke. He was in his sixth year as head coach of Luke and I trusted his judgment. I went to him in the spring of my senior year.

"Well, Sonny," he said, "your game plan is a good one. I like that you're thinking about your future. And frankly, I think you might have what it takes to play JC ball and maybe, just maybe, at a higher level. But I didn't play college, and that never deterred me from chasing a coaching career." He leaned over his desk. "I enjoy coaching here in Luke, and we've done some good things, but I, like you, have aspirations of climbing the coaching ladder. But, I must tell you, it's not easy. It's highly political."

I nodded.

"I have two thoughts," he said. "For one thing, why sell yourself short? Why not try for a football scholarship?"

"I didn't think any schools would offer," I said.

"Sonny, you never know until you try," he said.

"So, what should I do?"

"Well," said Coach Tripp, "you have film, right?"

I mentioned my cousin's film of the ninety-nine yard run.

"I can send that film off to Blinn and the JCs here in the Panhandle. Try for a scholarship, and if that fails, you can walk on then."

"You think I'm good enough, coach?"

"I do. I know you're fast. You need about fifty pounds, but you're not done growing. And the college people will have you in the weight room."

"What," I asked, "was the other thing?"

"If you don't make it to the NFL as a coach, will that kill you?"

"It's my dream," I said.

"Consider," he said, "that if you don't make it that high, you can still coach somewhere. My plan is still a work in progress. And like I said earlier, this business of high school coaching is political and competitive. But coaches in this state, even at the high school level, especially in the big school divisions, are treated almost like small college coaches. They have cars, make good salaries, and if they don't win they get fired. So dream big because I know you can get to the top, but don't crater if you aren't coaching on Sunday. There's plenty out there for you."

I thanked Coach Tripp and left. I even envisioned him and I together on an NFL coaching staff. My toughest problem would be breaking the news to my parents. It would kill my dad. He was a lifetime farmer as were my granddad and my three uncles who operated farms in the area, one of the farms next door. But unlike my grandfather, and my uncles, my parents had but one child, that being me. So it was my parents' plan to work me into one day running our farm while they cut back. I didn't dislike farming. But my heart was in coaching. We were at dinner when I broke the news.

"Hell, Sonny," said my dad. "I love football same as the

next guy. Nobody gets more riled than I do when the Cowboys lose. But football produces nothing real. Nothing you can put your hands on. This place is yours, ready to walk onto. This is Mother Earth. Things grow here. Things we eat. Things that are life itself. We feed ourselves. We feed people. We help feed the world. Please don't walk away from this."

I knew the conversation would be tough. I looked at my mother seated across the table her head down.

"Have you thought this through, Sonny?" she asked, head still lowered.

"I have Mother," I said.

She sighed. "Well, okay then." She looked at my father. "John, it's what he wants to do. There's no begrudging a young man from following a dream. Let's leave this alone for another time. Let's eat our meal."

So, things went on through the spring. I got word from Coach Tripp that several junior colleges had shown interest, but one, Panhandle JC, said that though there were no full scholarships available, were I to walk on, a student loan could be arranged and, should I prove myself worthy, might be offered a full scholarship my second year.

This appealed to me. Panhandle was less than three hours away by car. I could come home on the weekends and help my parents. That might take some of the sting out of my decision not to take over the farm. I told Coach Tripp I was on board for Panhandle. I made application to the school both for admission and the loan. My parents were required to countersign both documents as, at the time, I was not yet eighteen years old.

My parents signed without so much as a word. I didn't play baseball or run track that spring. I felt guilty and made it a point to spend as much time around my parents and the farm as I could. But it was clumsy and apparent I was trying too hard to be the good son. I had never felt awkward around my parents before. Things were uncomfortable.

Then death intervened. Not six weeks before I was to graduate, my father passed away. It was as though the Divine was telling me I could not leave the farm. Dad had gone out to plow one of our forty-acre fields. We owned 160 acres, (a quarter section), and through hard work it had become a productive family enterprise.

That morning, my father, as was his practice, had driven along the gravel county road that formed one of the boundaries of our farm. There was a small patch of trees next to an old shed on the backside of the field where Dad had parked our tractor and plow. He left the car locked along the road and had walked to the tractor several hundred feet away. On days such as this, my mother, at around noon, would drive her car out to him with his lunch. That morning she found him on the ground next to his car, his face, neck, and arms red and swollen.

I was in town buying groceries. I had volunteered to help with the plowing, but as things had grown cold between my father and I, his silence spoke volumes when I offered my assistance. My mother suggested I take her car to town, and because of my grocery errand, she was about thirty minutes late that day getting out to my father.

My father had been stung to death by hornets. A rather large hive had grown in the shed, and, when my father mounted the tractor and started it up, the hive attacked him. Apparently he ran for his car, no doubt the hornets swarming him, but as he had done before, accidentally locked his keys in the car. He was forty-seven.

I couldn't leave my mother alone. She made it clear to me that she could take care of herself. My uncles in the area could farm our place with her maintaining the house. But she and my dad had been inseparable. In her way, she was strong. She had a wiser view of life than did my father. But emotionally, she relied on him heavily.

I called Coach Tripp and informed him of my situation.

He understood fully. I also contacted the Panhandle's athletic director who said to get back with him in a year if things worked out.

I took over the farm. For a while I kept my dream of coaching in the NFL alive, but as the years went by it was as though someone made that plan that I used to know.

My remaining on the farm gave my mother peace of mind that naturally made me feel good. She once asked me if I was angry with her for holding me back but I assured her I was right where I wanted to be. She wanted grandkids, something she had mentioned numerous times when I was in high school. But the derailment of my coaching career had silenced her on that.

Ten years went by in a blink. I was busy, not only with the physical labor that farming entailed, but with the business end of it—the books, paying seasonal help, talking to our accountant. I was the man of the family and the head of a stout farming operation. I was neither happy nor unhappy, but I was getting lonely. Then Pam Banks and I connected.

I was four years older than Pam, me twenty- eight, her twenty- four. She and I had both been in Luke High School together, but I had paid her no attention. When I was a senior, she was a freshman who had simply not caught my eye.

But after going away to college (Texas Tech in Lubbock) she had returned to Luke with a degree in education and a personal interest in art. Our families knew each other casually through church, school, and business. Her dad, Elmer Banks, ran the local feed store.

Pam was easy to look at. She had two sisters, good looking as well, all three girls taking after their red headed mother. The girls (mom included) were spirited types who kept Elmer working hard at keeping them happy. My mother once referred to Marjorie Banks and her three girls as "high maintenance."

Pam had returned to Luke after dropping out of law

school in Lubbock. She had taken a teaching job in our elementary school, and, now that I look back from a distance, was probably a bit lost. We met at church. I asked her out on a date and she accepted. Admittedly, she mesmerized me. Bear in mind that prior to meeting Pam, I had never had a steady girl friend. There were opportunities, especially in high school, my athletic prowess getting me plenty of female attention. But as the years faded, and the girls from the area had married and moved on, I became somewhat a loner, a status in life that concerned my mother, whose opinion of Pam in my life was mixed.

Nevertheless, despite a mild warning from my mother, who I believe was still feeling as though she had ruined my life and therefore would not interfere, Pam and I married. We moved into town, buying a cute little house with a detached garage that Pam immediately turned into an art studio. Pam's drive to her teaching job was a short one, and I drove daily to the farm where mother had left my bedroom completely intact.

Things went well for five years. Pam, much to my mother's dismay, did not want children. She made that clear prior to marriage. And I, who had begun thinking about a family, let it go by. It was in the fourth year of our marriage that mother died. I was thirty-two years old at the time. I had been tuning our tractor (a new one since the death of my father) and was on my way to the house for a drink of water when I saw my mother collapse in her garden. She was bending over, a watering pot in her left hand, when she staggered and clutched her right hand to her chest. She was dead on the spot, having lived sixty years, the last fourteen heartbroken.

One night, a year later, I was doing the books in our kitchen. Pam was out back, in her studio, working on one of her wildlife paintings. In my view, she was actually quite good. I was toying with the idea of Pam and I selling the house in town and us moving out to the farm. There was an old smoke house we could turn into her art studio, or we could simply keep the house in town as guesthouse while she kept the studio there. It all seemed workable to me.

But just as death and love had changed my path, heartbreak did as well. Pam came into the kitchen, nodded to me, and then after a brief cup of coffee (she offered me one as well) sat down at the table with me, my business records forming a small barrier between us.

"Sonny," she said. "I'd like to talk."

I knew her voice. I knew most things about her. She was, after all, my wife. This was serious.

"What is it, Pam?" I asked.

"I want a divorce."

I leaned back into my chair taking in the statement.

"I didn't see this coming," I said. "I take it you're unhappy."

"I am," she sighed. "Sonny, it's not you. It's Luke. I've outgrown this place."

"You're bored," I said. "We can change that"

"I don't think so," she said.

"So, you're not in love with me anymore," I stated.

She looked away a bit, trying to keep eye contact with me.

"I'm sorry, Sonny. I really am."

So things ended between Pam and me. It was friendly and painless. Pam was not greedy. She wanted nothing of the farming business. She asked for a bit of seed money which, coupled with an amount she received from Elmer, would get her started in Dallas (her chosen destination) where she would teach, paint and start over. There was no "other man." She simply wanted a change without me. We sold the house in town, letting her keep most of that. She moved on. Our parting kiss was lukewarm, both of us holding back.

I went into a depression. I kept myself going through exhausting physical labor that helped me sleep at night. Here I was, thirty-three years old, alone, living a life I didn't want. I considered driving to Dallas and begging Pam to come back, but I knew it was over. I finally took stock of my life. In some respects, I wasn't that much different from Pam, wanting something different from life. Luke, Texas was not for me.

My cousin, Lon, had taken over my uncle's place, which bordered ours to the east. It was Lon who had filmed my ninety-nine yard run. He and I had always been close. I owned outright, after my mother's death, the entire farm of 160 acres. I offered Lon the chance to buy it. He and I sat down over my mother's kitchen table that had been in our house for as long as I could remember.

"I'd love to buy your place," said Lon, "but I couldn't borrow the money."

"You're credit's good," I stated.

"It is," said Lon, "but I'm over-collateralized on my other loans. I've tried three banks to get the next place over. You know I want Drew's farm?"

"No, I didn't know that."

"Well, I do. I'd love to get yours and his, but right now, I can't get either."

We parted. I toyed with going to a realtor and selling to any third party, but I had my parents in mind and I knew they would want me to keep the farm in the family. I came to Lon with a proposition.

"Lon, why not rent from me?"

"Will that work for you?" he asked.

"Yes," I said. "Give me the landlord's share every six months and I'll be happy. When you get your operation back up to speed, let me know, and we can talk about you buying it."

That plan worked. He and I shook on the deal. I told him he could use the house as a headquarters or a guesthouse. I didn't want him using it as a hunting lodge, however, as I didn't want my mother's home trashed. I wanted our home kept as it had been for forty years, but I also knew I might never be back, so I gave my three aunts (two by blood, one by marriage) permission to take whatever things had sentimental value to them. I also gave them permission, that, but for a few items, to hold an estate sale, the proceeds of which I would split with them. As executor of my mother's estate, I put approval to do all of that in writing.

I had no idea what I wanted to do. I decided to carve my new future in Houston. Pam was in Dallas, and I wanted no temptation to reunite with her cluttering my thinking.

I hit Houston with my Ford pickup and my life's savings of ten thousand dollars. I was the quintessential hillbilly. I was petrified on the Houston freeways. I'd experienced a bit of that kind of driving, but now, in the everyday of Houston life, I dreaded driving around town. People honked at me and shot me the finger when all I was doing was simply driving the speed limit.

I found a cheap apartment that, looking back, was in a rough part of town. I had no friends, so life was lonely. Thank God I wasn't a drinker or I would have retreated into the bottle for companionship.

I did construction work for six months, but realized I hadn't come to Houston to lift rocks and lumber. I tried selling tractors for John Deere and discovered a liking for sales (it turns out I'm a "people" guy), but I was new to the selling game and, to my dismay, was let go when the economy slowed down. Big city life was a different animal, but I also had my ace in the hole, that being crop checks from cousin Lon coming every six months. Like clockwork, I received personal checks, usually in the amount of ten thousand dollars, in the mail in January and July. I had enough to sustain me at a very meager standard of living.

Then I stumbled into the Georgellen Club. I had never seen the ocean. And, true, the Gulf of Mexico was not technically such, but to me water as far as you could see was "the ocean." I took a drive to Galveston to kill an afternoon and, since it was lunchtime, stopped in for a meal. I sat on the outside deck on a beautiful March afternoon, eating a cheeseburger, washing it down with unsweetened iced tea, listening to the waves roll gently onto the beach. It was a new and soothing sound for me.

I took a liking to Galveston and especially to the club where a weekly visit helped me relax and reassure myself that my life would eventually work out. I was sitting on the deck that next summer, having cashed one of Lon's checks, estimating a permanent move to Galveston when I met Dolph Hurley.

"I sell used cars," said Hurley. The club was spilling over with Fourth of July business and he walked up and asked if we could share a table. "Some people look upon that as a shady profession," he said, "and it can be if you're not honest. But you can ask anybody on the island what they think of my cars and you'll find very few have anything negative to say about me." He pointed to a handsome young waiter scampering between tables. "And, I've managed to feed my wife and three boys, that waiter being one of them, rather well. His two brothers are in college at A&M, and if I could get through to him, he'd be there too. But, in any case, if you combine honest hard work with a sound used car, there's absolutely nothing wrong with that occupation." He took an enormous bite from a corned beef sandwich then launched into a colorful history of a professional baseball career. When he left, he picked up the tab, leaving his business card. "You probably figured out that I'm looking for a salesman. If you know anyone, have them call me." He looked me directly in the eye.

If I was going to make the Galveston move, I would need a job. I knew that if cars were anything like tractors (having tuned many), I could sell them. I called Dolph Hurley who had me drop by his lot that was a mile or so west of the Georgellen Club. We had a nice talk, I told him I was moving to Galveston, and was itching to work. He hired me.

The next ten years were a blur. Dolph taught me the used car business. I took to it like a fish to water. I made Dolph money. Patronizing the Georgellen Club was a boon to business. I ate lunch there every day. I got to know people — waiters, teachers, construction workers, fishermen, even tourists who were summer regulars to the Island. The club was a second office for me.

One day, while in an exceptionally good mood, I began flirting with Connie Torres. I was forty-five years old, and I figured Connie for ten years younger than me. As it turns out, she was a young looking forty. Connie was a waitress at the club who had been waiting on me for several years. She was cute as a bug. It took me a while, but I asked her out to dinner. Despite my failed marriage with Pam, I had not sworn off women.

Connie and I hit it off. She was fiery, which I liked. I admit to comparing her to Pam, who was educated and at times could pontificate. Connie was pure, down to earth working class. Things heated up between us and, on one of our dates (away from the Georgellen Club) we threw our cards on the table. I candidly told her of my past, Pam included, and of my aborted coaching dream. She gave me her story as well.

"I'm a convicted felon," she said. "Did you know that?"

"No," I said.

"Does that alarm you?"

"I haven't decided yet. Tell me."

Connie launched into her story. She held nothing back. And though it hurt her to tell me, I could see that brutal honesty was part of her personality.

"I killed my baby," she said, "should I keep going?"

"Yes," I answered, and so she did.

"I met a guy named Mike Bull when I was eighteen. I was a good student in high school, but I didn't want college. I was in technical school. I was studying to be an inhalation therapist."

"He was a student?" I asked.

"I met him in a bar" she said. "He was an outlaw. If there was a rule, he needed to break it. Him and me shacked up. He liked to get high. I should have seen him coming but I wouldn't look past the thrill. Before long him and me were selling coke and marijuana. We got high. We made money by selling drugs. I did office work. The inhalation therapist thing went out the window. We had a kid."

"We can stop here," I said.

"No," she said, "we need to do this. We got high one night and forgot we left Rene out on the porch. We were in an apartment with a small courtyard. We went inside for a second to smoke and next thing I knew it was morning and a neighbor was pounding on the door. The baby was out all night. It got cold and that was it. I did five years in the Crain unit. Mike did a full ten in Huntsville. It was an accident but I was his mother and I let him down when he needed me."

"Where's Bull?" I asked.

"He's dead. And that's good. He was coming around again and I don't know that I had it in me to tell him to go away. There, you know all about me. Are we strong or does this end it for us?"

"My ex-wife got bored," I said. "I've got no Mike Bull in me. I bring no excitement to the table."

"I'm not looking for another Mike Bull."

We got married in a Catholic ceremony by a priest friend of the Torres family. It was small, me, Connie, her mother and two aunts. Her father was dead, and her sister didn't attend. Her mother and aunts liked me once they realized I was a good citizen. Connie made clear before we got married that she wanted no children. Once upon a time I did, but at my age I'd lost interest.

Things clicked right along for a few more years. I turned fifty. I was selling cars and enjoying it. Connie stayed waitressing at the Georgellen Club. She was a worker at heart and stayed loyal to Tom York who hired her when she was at bottom. About that time, Dolph Hurley came to me with an offer. We sat down to lunch in the Georgellen Club.

"Sonny," he said, "I'll get right to the point. I'm looking to sell the lot. I'm willing to give you first bite. You interested?"

And I was. But I didn't have the money. Dolph's lot sat on land that was worth more as a resort than it was as a used car lot. Lon was still sending me money twice a year, but this was big, not nickel and dime stuff. I passed on Dolph's offer. He sold out, as he should have, to a developer. After fifteen years of working with Dolph, I was out of a job. I knew I was at another crossroads. Connie and I were tighter than ever so there was no immediate pressure for me to find work. I took a step back and decided to look for an opportunity, a big one. It came in the form of a bankrupt car dealership on the Gulf Freeway, south of Houston. It was going for pennies on the dollar, but, once again, money was the problem. I tried a few lenders but none believed in me. Then I got a call from Lon that for all I know might have been divine intervention.

"You still want to sell me your home place?" asked Lon.

I hadn't been back to Luke but two or three times in the last fifteen years, and only then to visit Lon and make a quick pass by our farm. Lon had been a good steward which didn't surprise me. He had painted, with my permission, our house. Inside, but for the items taken out by my aunts, the home was as my parents had kept it. There was nothing for me in Luke and, frankly, it hurt to go back.

"You couldn't have called at a better time," I said.

Lon and I struck a fair deal. I sold him our place, lock, stock and barrel for one hundred sixty thousand dollars, which was the appraised value. I could have gotten more, but Lon had shot square with me, and he and I were like brothers. I put the money down on the dealership and with that, got the loan I needed to buy it.

I was never so hungry in life for success. Part of me wanted to cross paths one day with Pam and show her what I had become. But I reminded myself how lucky I was to have Connie. I got my ego back under control.

My dealership took off. And how could it not? The location was terrific. I hired good people, sales and service, who I paid well and gave good benefits to. Both Connie and I were working people and we knew happy employees who worked hard were the key to success. I'm a hands-on owner. I'm at the lot every Monday through Saturday, from early in the morning to closing. I walk the lot every day. In that respect I'm guilty of micro managing, which is the frugal farm boy in me. Other than that, I think I'm a good fellow to work for.

Connie insisted on keeping her job at the Georgellen Club despite us having more money than we could spend. She would not allow herself to lose touch with hard work. I'm comfortable with that. Working keeps us both happy and glad to see each other.

One Saturday in November, several years into owning the dealership, I decided to take the afternoon off. I called Connie and let her know what I was up to. I'd read in the Houston paper that morning of a state semifinal playoff game in Rice stadium between two of the big school teams in the state. I hadn't been to a live football game in three decades. I drove to the stadium, parked my car and strolled in.

It was a beautiful day, a football day. The sky was dark blue, no clouds, and at noon the temperature was chilly, but seated in the sun, I felt just right. I sat at the forty yard line by myself, watching Rice stadium fill.

When the two teams came out I wandered to the end zone where I watched one of the teams warm up. Players at the 5A level were huge and the size of the squad numbered at least sixty. It was Texas high school football at its best.

I saw a coach walking amongst the players as they stretched. It was Coach Tripp who I hadn't seen in thirty years. He was as lean as ever, but bald. His voice seemed deeper as he shouted out encouragement.

"Coach Tripp," I yelled, "Coach Bob Tripp. Luke, Texas says 'hello'!"

He turned to look up at me. I had changed. I was thirty pounds heavier and the burr haircut I had in high school was gone, replaced by combed hair. I wore glasses in high school. Now I wore contact lenses. He squinted, looking into the sun that silhouetted me.

"Who are you?" he asked.

"Sonny," I yelled. "Sonny Hughes!"

I watched as his mind scrolled. Then, "I'll be doggoned!"

He motioned me toward a wooden gate at the base of the concrete fence encircling the stadium. I opened it and he let me in the end zone. At first he wanted to hug me but he caught himself and thrust out his hand.

"Sonny, God it's good to see you. You have no idea how many times over the years I've thought about you."

That made me feel good. Coach Tripp had been a second father to me. I held back tears. We talked for fifteen minutes. I had followed his career up through the Texas schoolboy ranks to its highest level. I told him so.

"No, Coach Tripp, I never made it into coaching," I said when he asked.

"Do you regret that?" he asked.

"Sometimes, a little," I said. "But it's getting farther away from me. It's turned out well. I've had a good life."

We broke it off. We mentioned briefly staying in touch. I went back into the stands; Coach Tripp back to his team. The game started. It was hard, clean, Texas football. Midway through the third quarter, with the game tied, Coach Tripp's fullback, a big fast white boy with college potential, broke clean from the line of scrimmage. As the fullback pulled away, I was taken back for an instant to a Friday night long ago in Luke Texas, players in pursuit, and me running like hell without a care in the world.

The Cook

Life. Go figure. It's all about choices. I made a bad one. And I paid for it. This is how it happened.

When I was eighteen, a senior in a Catholic boy's high school, a fellow student named Nick Moore and I got it into our heads that we were a pair of bad-asses. We were anything but that. We were middle class white boys who had been raised by concerned parents. We went to good schools. Our home training was exemplary. We wanted for nothing. And yet, there we were, acting like gangsters with our affected walk and talk.

Nick and I skipped school on a Friday afternoon in February, three months before we were to graduate. We were both headed to college, him locally, me, out of state. We were reasonably bright but you wouldn't know it if you'd crossed paths with us in 1968.

Nick had a car, and I had money. I kept a small savings account at a neighborhood bank amounting to a couple of hundred dollars I earned each of the previous two summers as a lifeguard. So on that Friday we decided to pull some money from my account and take a ride into Houston to see about picking up some hookers in the seedy Montrose area.

Then fate intervened. This is where, looking back, I realize that one seemingly insignificant thing can turn into a life-changing event. I withdrew one hundred dollars from my account (Nick was in the car) and on my way out walked several feet behind a well-dressed man who looked to be in his forties. He wore a suit and a tie, what I would think of today as a professional. At one point he held the door for me. I gave him my tough guy nod. As we were walking across the asphalt parking lot to our respective cars I noticed a small piece of paper fall from his pants pocket. I picked it up thinking I would signal him so as to return it. Before I could return it, Nick, who was within an arm's length of me, sitting in the driver's seat of his Camaro, the window down, said, "Wait, what is it?"

I showed it to him. There was nothing on the slip of paper that contained the man's name or address. Scribbled on it, however, was the number $70,000 which led me, and Nick, to believe the man had gotten that figure from the teller. Was it a deposit? Was it a withdrawal in the form of a check he was carrying? Was it an account balance? A domino had been tipped over.

A red corvette passed slowly before us, at its wheel the fellow whose piece of paper we held.

"Get his plates," said Nick.

I walked to the front of Nick's car where I looked casually to my left. I whispered audibly to Nick the letters and numbers on the corvette's license plate which Nick wrote down on the same slip of paper that held the large figure of money.

"This is big time," he said. "Can you believe this fell into our laps?"

There was a pay phone a few blocks over. Nick's cousin Gayle worked for the DMV. It was a simple task for him to call her and fabricate a story that had his car in a minor accident with a driver who fled the scene. If he furnished her with the license plate could she respond with a name and an address? That she did, thinking she had done her cousin a favor, not realizing our darker purpose.

Rather than buying whores, we went to a gun shop whereupon producing identification we purchased a cheap "Saturday Night Special" for fifty dollars and the ammunition to go along with it. I'd never fired nor held a gun, nor do I believe Nick had, but he had a swagger that convinced an indifferent salesman in the small dark shop that everything was on the level. It was two o'clock on Friday afternoon. We decided to go home as we normally would from school, eat dinner with our families, and then leave our houses at 5:30 under the ruse of going to our high school's basketball game that night. This we did, and at the agreed time Nick picked me up at the curb in the front of my house.

What were we going to do? We had no plan. And if the fellow had money did we really think we could handle a large sum? Nick produced a pair of bandanas from a paper bag on the front seat. Ski masks would have been the better choice. I think now that our false bravado made it impossible for either of us to back down from the incredibly poor path we were venturing down. As we drove toward our destination I found myself hoping Nick would call it off or that I would simply say, "I can't do this. Let me out." But neither of us said a word.

When we arrived at the address Gayle had given us it was dark. I looked at the clock on the Camaro's dash. It was 6:40. We sat for a minute, both of us breathing hard.

"So, we're for real on this?" asked Nick.

"I am if you are," I said.

We slid quietly out of the Camaro, but not before tying the bandanas around our necks. Nick rolled the barrel of the handgun trying, I'm convinced, to look authentic. There was a streetlight on a nearby corner that cast the front yard in a yellow glow. At the porch we pulled the bandanas above our noses so that only our eyes showed. Mine smelled of motor oil, like it had come from the floor of a garage. My nose itched but there was no taking down the bandana. Nick turned the doorknob of the front door. We stepped into a vestibule with a marbled floor. Off to the right was a small living room. It had a hard wood floor, an area rug, and a desk. There was the sound of television coming from the den at the end of the vestibule. From where I stood I could see the light of the television shifting on a wall. Something fried was in the air, maybe chicken.

"That you, Carla?" said a voice.

We waited. It would be easy to run out the front door, jump in the Camaro, and drive like hell. Nick's eyes looked at me from behind his bandana. I looked at the gun. It shook.

We turned the corner into the den, Nick in the lead. Seated on a yellow couch was the man from the bank whose withdrawal slip I had picked up.

"This is real," said Nick. "We're not fucking around!"

The fellow turned toward us as in an afterthought. I took a quick look at the television. A John Wayne movie was playing. Nick's gun hand was quivering.

"What do you want?" asked the man.

"This," said Nick. He tossed the bank slip on the couch near the man.

The man opened the crumpled paper as his eyes narrowed.

"Not gonna happen," he said.

"I know there's money here," said Nick. "Don't bullshit me."

"There's no money here. That's my account balance. Do you two punks really think I'd keep money like that lying around?" He looked directly at Nick's gun hand. "Go home. I'll pretend this never happened." He laughed and returned his attention to the John Wayne movie.

"I'm not asking again," said Nick. "There's money in here somewhere. I know it."

He put the revolver to the man's head.

"What are you going to do?" the man asked. He looked at me. I sensed he read me like a book. Nick was the alpha male. I was his weak follower.

"I'm gonna ask one more time," said Nick. He pulled back the gun's hammer.

"And I'm done being nice," said the man. "There's no money here. Now get out of my house because you're really pissing me off."

My life was changed right there. Nick pulled the trigger. I'll never know what he was thinking. A startled look passed over the man's face as he slumped onto the couch. The noise the gun made was loud. It rang in my ears. And I'd never smelled gun smoke before. There was a small hole in the man's right temple. A red chunk of matter had plopped onto the yellow throw pillow left of him.

"What did you do?" I asked.

"There's money here. I know it," said Nick.

We rifled through the desk in the living room and the drawer in the bedroom. A few minutes later we heard a voice come from the kitchen area "Brian, help me with the groceries. Brian, whose car is parked out front? Is someone here?"

Nick and I walked quietly to the front door. I wondered what would happen if the female voice walked into the den. Coming from the kitchen I heard the sound of paper crumbling. Nick and I made it through the front door.

Once in the Camaro I said, "Don't look back. Just drive."

The next day we were arrested at school. It was quick and quiet. The police accosted Nick and me coming out of our civics class. Somebody from the neighborhood watch had gotten the plates. We got cuffed and read our rights. Nick tried to look tough but his lower lip was jumping. I felt small.

From downtown I called my parents. They wouldn't believe what I told them. They showed up with a lawyer. She told me to say nothing. I took her advice. An hour later she came back with a deal. We would *both* be charged with capital murder which carried with it the death penalty or mandatory life in prison or *one* of us would get the capital charge and I, if I talked, could get the lesser charge of first degree murder which had neither the death penalty nor the mandatory life sentence. I would, however, be looking at sixty years, subject to possible parole in twenty years. I sang like the proverbial choirboy.

Nick got a life sentence without parole. He ducked the death penalty. A jury, with testimony from parents and friends, didn't figure him for a continuing threat to society. I took my sixty years, a span of time beyond my comprehension. I never saw Nick again and didn't care.

I went into prison two days after my nineteenth birthday. Let me put it this way, there were things I did those first ten years to survive that I don't want to talk about. By the time I was thirty I wasn't virgin meat anymore so prison life wasn't quite so threatening. I figured I should make good use of my time. I read when I could. I finished high school in prison then went on to earn a college degree (correspondence) in English. I was rather competent in sentence structure to begin with so that degree came easy. And I put it to use. With the warden's permission I taught inmates to read. At first only a few were interested, but over the years the group grew and eventually I conducted three classes a week. The inmates loved it. They gained purpose from it. Becoming literate not only opened them up to ideas, but it gave them a deeper understanding of themselves. The warden appreciated it. He received kudos for it. Gang violence subsided. I had all colors learning to read: Asians, Blacks, Latinos, Anglos. They didn't become friends, but in my classes they recognized a desire for literacy as a shared goal.

I met Perry Young in one of the classes. His "prison" name was Fat Young and for good reason. He was less than six feet tall but weighed, I'm sure, near four hundred pounds.

Obesity aside, he was incredibly strong, and with his mass, no one provoked him. He was also the cook. He ran the kitchen. You don't want a cook angry at you while you're in prison. Not when he controls what goes in your stomach.

He was a polite guy, and actually a good reader, who wanted to better himself. He took a liking to me and invited me into the kitchen as an assistant cook. I wasn't going anywhere soon. The widow of the man Nick and I killed attended my parole hearing and brought along with her quite an entourage. They convinced the board, that, despite my accomplishments in prison, I hadn't paid enough for the loss of her husband. I also liked the idea of learning a trade just in case I ever got paroled.

Fat (that's what he preferred) was a good teacher. He started me out slow, dicing, peeling, then frying and boiling simple things. I learned how to cook for a large group, seasoning my dishes to accommodate a wide variety of appetites. I knew going in that I would enjoy cooking and the experience was wonderful. Some nights I would lie awake in my cell thinking about what I had accomplished in prison knowing that I had missed a true opportunity at a good productive life in the outside world.

That life went on for another eleven years. I was forty. Fat, himself in prison for life, ("I'm a contract killer, not a serial killer, let's be clear on that," he said) suffered a massive heart attack one day in the kitchen. I saw him go. It wasn't slow. One second he was stirring that night's beef stew, and then he gasped and clutched his chest, hitting the concrete floor without interruption so hard that hot soup splashed out of a serving bowl. I suspect he was dead before he hit the ground.

In those eleven years that I knew him, I met his daughter and grandson during their visits. I'd lost both of my parents in the previous decade, in my mind primarily from heartbreak, so on those occasions Fat had me sit with him, Sandy (his daughter) and Roy (his grandson.) I was flattered and actually a bit moved that he thought me worthy of such an invitation. Despite his background, Fat was very proud and protective of those two. One day, in the kitchen, he had pulled me off to the side and requested that, should I ever make it to the outside, would I be so kind as to look out for them as his wife was dead and Sandra's husband had also met his fate (information I did not pursue.) I promised him I would do that which produced a peaceful look across his massive bald head.

I finally made parole. And, truthfully, I was in no great hurry to get out. I was fifty-nine years old and had done a full forty years. Despite that time being spent in prison, it had all gone by rather quickly. I had seen people come, go and come back again. I became somewhat of a historian, telling stories to the new inmates about legendary characters who had done their time. I was on my third warden, the other two, both decent fellows, retired and dead. The third warden, a youngish looking fellow in his forties, found out for me, (I was curious in my old age) that Nick Moore had died, victim of a stroke, in the prison (not mine) he had spent his entire life.

My parole officer was a woman named Rusk. She was all business, which I appreciated. Other than my mother and Fat's daughter, I had not spoken to a female in forty years. Rusk sat across from me in her office. I'd say she was about my age and had seen enough of life to not be fooled by bullshit. She wasn't bad looking. She was tall for a woman, dressed like a man in business attire, with short brown hair. I picked up the scent of what I remembered as perfume. I wondered what I would do with a woman in my life. The whole idea of living in the outside world was overwhelming. It crossed my mind to violate parole so as to get sent back. I had no one on the outside, and life had passed me by.

"You were a cook," she said as she read my file.

"I was," I answered.

"And you graduated college while in prison."

"I did that too."

"So, what do you want to do?" she asked.

"Go back to prison."

"Well," she said, "I'm not sending you back unless you mess up. And odds are you will. But before you do, my advice is to get a taste of what you've missed out on for forty years. Here." She handed me a slip of paper with a name and a phone number.

"Call this guy," she said. "He might have something for you."

I made a phone call the next morning from Sandra Young's kitchen. She had picked me up the morning I was released and let me sleep on her couch until I found a job and got on my feet. The man I met was Tom York, owner of the Georgellen Club. I had never interviewed for a job in my life. The lifeguarding job I had in high school was through a friend so the job was basically given to me. But I'd been in front of a parole board three times so I sort of knew the drill. I dressed in a pair of slacks and a collared, short-sleeved shirt along with a pair of wing tips all of which Sandra helped me pick out at Good Will.

"Diane Rusk worked here once," said York "so if she recommends you, I'll listen."

He looked at the application on his desk. We sat across from each other at a table in the Georgellen Club that had not yet opened for the day. "What can you cook?"

"Just about anything," I said. "I can go short order or I can make a full course meal. I've put together Thanksgiving and Christmas meals with all the fixings for inmates and I've fried hamburgers and pancakes. I've worked with poultry, fish, beef and pork. I like cooking. I like the creative part about it."

"Can you handle a schedule?"

"You mean showing up for work on time?"

"That's what I mean," said York.

"Well, if prison is anything," I said, "it's structure. In fact, if I have trouble on the outside, it will be because I won't know what to do during those times there is no structure, if that makes sense."

York eyeballed my arms.

"No drugs or alcohol problems?" he asked.

"None," I said. "Never smoked, drank, or touched drugs. And I don't intend to start now."

"No tattoos, I see," said York as he continued to look at my arms.

"My mother didn't like tattoos. I ruined her life and my dad's as well. It was the least I could do for her."

"I remember your crime," said York "you and I are about the same age."

"I did a horrible thing. I helped kill a man. I took his life, destroyed the lives of his wife, my parents, and God knows whom else. Apologizing won't change anything. So all I can do is lead a good life from here on in. I was a model prisoner. I understood fully that I did a great deal of damage. I doubt I can ever fathom the degree."

I got the job from Tom York. The job, in Galveston, took me out of Harris County where my parole was being administered. Sandra, Roy and I moved to the far reaches of south Harris County, just inside the county line, into an apartment that was about a twenty minute drive from the Georgellen Club. Sandra continued to drive me to work as I was in no shape to handle a car on the Houston freeway. I had a car in high school, but not driving for forty years had taken its toll on my reflexes and nerves.

Sandra, Roy and I became somewhat of an informal family. I started sleeping with Sandra, and shortly thereafter she and I got married through a justice of the peace. Sandra and Roy were honest, kind people which surprised me since their patriarch had been a contract killer. But I suppose people are capable of leading public and private lives apart from one another.

On one of my days off I asked Sandra to drive me past my boyhood home. We drove by and parked for a few minutes. My parents were long dead. I imagined my mother working in her flowerbed while my dad mowed the yard, his car parked in the driveway.

One foolish mistake. All that time wasted.

The Boxer

Mamma teach me how save coin, not Daddy. Daddy work hard but I learns all about money from Mamma—how to turns penny into dime and dime into dollar. She say don't be trusting no bank. Bank take farm and house and people dreams away. Sometime you try pull saving out, it be gone too. Mamma don't be able read or write good but she understand thing. She tell me all about grow up in Raleigh. Grandpa Leon loose his farm. Grandma Lucille eyes swell up she cry so bad. Mamma and Uncle James live in flatbed truck for two week until they finds rent house. Mamma teach me other things too; put can food away in pantry so you eats when life go bad and family be all you has.

I tries real hard. I sees Thurston and Daddy be sitting in living room watch TV. Mamma be sleep on sofa her shoes off. We be in Memphis. Daddy don't be working at airline yet. Him and Mamma still be talking nice each other.

Then we moves to Houston. Daddy go work at airport load luggage. Mamma clean houses. Thurston be seventeen. I be seven. Thurston always complain he miss Memphis. Daddy get him job with airline wash down airplane but that not good enough. One day, Thurston leave. He don't say anything. I don't hears from Thurston in long time.

I works at Georgellen Club. I parks car. It be first job I has after box. Fifteen year go by fast. You asks me fifteen year ago I be here this long, I say you some kind of fool. Georgellen Club job pay good. I don't says great, I says good. Good night, I makes one hundred dollar in tip. Good week, I makes five, maybe six hundred dollar.

Plenty good looking womens come Georgellen Club. I don't be brag, but I gets my chances. I be in good shape. I takes care of myself. I have good body forty year old man. I weighs 218 pound. My fight weight be 212 pound. I get lady car, she say "Here my number. We haves fun sometime." I say "Thank you. You nice lady." Little devil be whisper my ear say "Why you don't go fuck that? Man give up whole life fuck that at night. She give it you free." Little angel say "Tucker, you knows not put dick in strange lady." Little angel sound lot like mamma.

I go gym two time week. Gym be my church. I be holy in gym. I go gym, I remembers who I is. I walks in, say hello to Timmy Burns. Timmy be at gym many year. Timmy wrap my hands. Timmy wrap you hand, he treat you like champ. Timmy treat everybody respect. My hand be hard now. I box, they be soft as lady hand. Timmy Burns talk real fast. Got mouth like machine gun. Words come out Timmy Burn like bullet. Timmy talk, I keeps mouth shut.

Timmy done, I goes to work on heavy bag. Bag feel like man. I hits bag, it shake. I young, I throws big right hook. Hook put you sleep I hits you. I hits bag again. Hit bag right, not many thing feel better. I crouches low. Elbows be tuck. I snorts like bull. My punches be hard. Knuckles be burning.

I be young, mind wander. Wander mind be my nature. Mr. Jake tell me many time good fighter be one who concentrate. I young, I get by be strong. Something inside me scream, want out. Mr. Jake always like my heart. He say heart be best part of me. Head be thing get me in trouble. Mr. Jake yell at me plenty time. I thinks I be in Rocky movie he yell so much.

Pink scar be over my left eye. I be eleven, I runs into Mamma rosebush. It good Mamma never see me box. Mamma strong. She tell people what she think. She wrong, she say so. She see me get hit, she don't let me box.

I gets hit plenty time. Black man from Mobile hit me left side face. He end my career. Pain go through me like big wave. I talks funny three day. Finger on right hand go numb. Mr. Jake tell me give it up.

I moves one side. I bounces on feet. I hits heavy bag harder. Chicago Sally walk by. He be wrinkle old man. Sally got one good eye. Why he call hisself Chicago I don't know. I guess he from Chicago. I never calls myself fancy ring name. What good it do I calls myself "Sugar" or "Hurricane" I don't be no good? Name don't make fighter good.   Plenty old fighter hang out in gym. They carry towel. They tell story things happen long time ago. They gots nothing better do. I worries that become me.

Two young heavyweight jump in center ring. One be colored boy. Skin be like rubber. Other boy be Mexican. "CHEO" be tattooed his left arm. Black be bigger man. Mexican boy be fast. Day it end for me Mr. Jake take me off to side. He say I need find new way make living. I be mad at Mr. Jake. I think he give up on me. Time go by, I gets past it. Mr. Jake right. I be done. I be as far as I go in ring.

I pulls off gloves. Hands be sweaty. Ray Cannon walk up. Ray be my corner man whole time I box pro. Best I knows, Ray have no regular woman. He got no family. All Ray Cannon have be fight game. It be Mr. Jake tell me I done boxing. I believe it be Ray Cannon put idea Mr. Jake head.

Ray be good man. Everybody upset, be crazy, Ray be calm. Room be loud, Ray walk in, room get low. Ray box pro ten year. He box middleweight. Ray say every fight be career. Every round be fight. Every punch be round. He say every mile, every sit up, every drop sweat be behind punch. Ray be detail man. He drive you crazy be so picky. He not miss anything. You lies to Ray, he know.

"How Tucker Kellogg?" ask Ray.

"Fine," I says.

"No you not," say Ray.

You see what I means about Ray?

"How Ray be?" I asks.

"Fine," laugh Ray. "Can't fuck. Too old. Can't eats what I likes. Got the diabetes. See. I be fine."

Ray and me watches. Black land good right hand Mexican ear. Mexican boy back up. He shake punch, start move. Feet be moving real fast now.

"What you think these two?" ask Ray.

"Colored boy got good knuckle game," I says.

"Black boy hit you," say Ray, "you change career. Mexican boy be better fighter."

What come Ray mouth I hear many time.

"Black be one punch fighter. He get lucky, hit you, he win. He don't get lucky, he get beat. Who you knows like that?"

I don't says nothing.

"You wins 15 fight. You loses 5 fight. You on brink of serious," say Ray.

Ray like get under my skin. Ray corner plenty of boxer his life. He make whole living in corner. Ray still know Tucker Kellogg record. That what I likes about Ray Cannon.

"I knows that," I says.

"What you best fight?" ask Ray.

"Puerto Rico boy in Buffalo. Purse be good."

"That not you best fight," say Ray.

"It not?"

"No," say Ray. "Best fight you first fight. That back when you listen me. You does what I tells you. You know you worst fight?"

"Mobile," I says.

"Nope," say Ray. "Worst be in Buffalo. Puerto Rican."

"Why you says that?"

"You win with bad habit," say Ray. "You win lucky punch. After Buffalo, you don't hears a word I say. You lose Mobile fight in Buffalo."

I don't argue Ray. I knows he be right.

"You want say 'Hi' Mr. Jake?" ask Ray.

"Sure," I says "where he at?"

Ray nod to end of ring. Mr. Jake be in metal chair. He look up at fighter in ring. He stare real hard.

"He got the dementia," say Ray.

"He do? Where he get that?" I asks.

"It creep up on him. It come four, five year. Long as he know this boxing I brings him."

We walks over Mr. Jake.

"Look who I has here," say Ray.

Mr. Jake look up at me.

"I hope you sorry ass be ready for Reno," he say. "We got big payday on way."

Ray tap me with his right foot.

"Mr. Jake. It me. Tucker Kellogg," I says.

"Don't do no good," say Ray. "He in different world."

Ray put hand on Mr. Jake back, work muscle at back of neck.

"Life be wunaful," he say while he rub. "Life be wunaful."

"I sees you later," I says.

Ray nod.

Couple month go by. Three, maybe four. Who count? Life be day on day. I goes work. I parks car. Two day week I goes gym. I don't be seeing Ray Cannon around in while. Make me think Mr. Jake mind be full gone. I meets woman in laundry room my building. Part of me say it be accident. Part of me know

I be on lookout. Woman name Kay Jackson. She got nice smile. She don't be pretty as Georgellen Club womens. Kay a little heavy. She say, "Why you don't be married?"

"How you knows I don't be married?" I asks.

She point to shirt I be wearing.

"No woman let her man out house in wrinkle shirt."

So, I starts seeing Kay. Just like that. Forty year old, I be by self. Now I gots woman. Kay work at cafeteria. She got life plan. First, she in night school finish her high school diploma. Kay tell me thing about her life. She call that share. She say people see each other they shares thing each other life. I tells her about Thurston go away. Not see him many year. Too many year count. I tell her I think I sees Thurston one time my fight he be sitting in first row. Then he be gone.

Kay other plan be go cook school. Kay want be world famous chef. She dream write cook book, have TV show. Kay believe strong in herself. You talk Kay, you believes in her too.

Kay get pregnant high school. First husband be long gone. Kay mamma and daddy help raise Kay child. They eyes tell truth. They not trust me.

Howard be Kay son. He fifteen. He big for his age. He start be trouble in school.

" You be doing my mamma?" he ask.

" I be true with you," I says, "I sleeps your mamma. But that no way talk you mamma. I don't talks my mamma that way. She dead. I misses her. She work hard whole life raise me. You mamma work hard too. She raise you."

"You respects my mamma, why you don't marries her?"

"She and me in stage we sees what happen. It not easy."

"Why not?" ask Howard.

"I be forty. You mamma be thirty-three. She be married before. I be set my way. I don't be used tell peoples where I goes or what I does."

"You teach me box?" Howard ask.

"I will" I says. "But it don't be so you beats peoples up. I teach you a little. See how you treats it."

Howard look at me real serious. He listen hard.

"You learn box," I says, "people leaves you alone."

"How people know that?" ask Howard.

"Man know boxer. Boxer got rhythm about him. About way he walk. About way he carry self. Ring never leave boxer. Ring be in his head. Be in his soul. Fighter feet be music. Hip be music. I walks down street, million peoples come by, be one boxer in whole crowd people, I spots him. Nobody fool with fighter. Man hit at boxer, he fool." I holds out my hands. "You sees these?"

"Yeah," say Howard.

"These be weapon. These hurt man bad he don't know box. These break rib. These hurt brain. These kill peoples. I teach you box, you be man with these hands. You don't be punk."

Me and Kay have regular thing. Sunday we eats roast beef and mashed potato at Kay apartment. We sits in Kay kitchen at small table. Whole time I eat I thinks. Getting old scare me. Mr. Jake lose mind scare me. Kay scare me too. Kay love me. Kay say she see good in me. She reach out her hand, touch mine. Her skin be smooth. It smell sweet.

"You more than old fighter, Tucker. Much more. Howard think world of you. Howard adore picture you give him." She lean across table, whisper, "So do I."

Kay make me feel thing I don't want feel. Thing I can't put in word. I squeezes her hand. I waits before I talks. I want pick my words right. I tells self Kay be alright things don't work out us. After Kay husband leave it take her long time feel okay again. She say that behind her now. She want get on with her life.

"You wants more to eat, Tucker?" she ask.

"No," I says.

" Dessert? I have peach pie," she ask.

" Maybe we don't sees each other no more," I says.

"Why you don't want see me?" ask Kay.

"I has no future, Kay. I parks cars. I be forty year old. I never be married. I don't knows nothing about kids."

Words feel funny come out of my mouth. Sound like they be floating on air. Not Tucker Kellogg word.

"You know why you be so hard to understand, Tucker?"

"No."

"You spend most of you life get hit by men who could kill you but you be scared to death of me and my boy. What make you think I wants to get married anyway?" Her face be blank but eyes be clear and simple.

"I'll tells you what," she say, "I don't brings marriage up. Ever. OK? Has I yet? Just promise me you won't run away from me because you be scared."

A few seconds goes by. "I be able manage that," I says. "Now what we do?"

Later we steps out of Kay shower. I drip water on her carpet. In mirror my back look like shiny map full of river and stream. Howard spend night with his grandparents. Have Kay in her bed still make me nervous.

"Why you stop?" she groan.

"I thought I be hurting you," I says.

She laugh. I know she don't be laughing at me. "OK," she say. "Keep hurt me."

* * *

Man got to change. Man don't change, life be full of empty. Whole time I box I don't make change. Every fight start out slow, steady. Middle round, other fighter make change. Late round, I lose fight. I fight same way even if corner say fight different. You don't make change at right time in ring, knockout or luck be only way you win fight. Now I sounds like Ray

94

Cannon.

I listens three people my life. I listen mamma. She be dead now. I listens Ray Cannon. Ray don't believe but I listens him. Not all time in ring. But I listens Ray outside ring. I listen Kay Jackson. Kay read motivate books. I tell her my plan start own business. Kay like my idea. She say first dream, then do. She say dream big, take little step.

"How long you dream own business?" she ask.

We be laying next each other Kay bed.

"Five year," I says.

"You hear blind man climb Mt. Ever?" she ask.

"No," I says.

"He be brave man."

"How he do it?" I asks.

"He have friend lead him. But he climb by hisself."

I closes my eyes try think climb mountain.

"He be my hero," say Kay. "I read book I thinks, put mind something I does it. Take step, climb mountain."

Kay remind me Ray Cannon. She push me way Ray push so I be better. Kay best thing happen me. Mamma like Kay she be alive. Tucker Kellogg dream be have limousine service. Take people airport. Dream come one night I be parking car at Georgellen Club. Kay help me see dream come true. Take step, climb mountain.

I walks onto car lot. Office be at back of lot. Two men in office. Man who own lot name Hurley. Hurley have big hand, fat cheek. He smile a lot. Other man be thin. He smoke cigar. He name Sonny. I be wearing money belt under my jacket. Belt be full. Everything I save be in that belt.

Some people good at many thing. Some people good at one thing. Some people good at nothing. I good park car. I good one time in ring. Smart thing do, man know what he good at, what he not good at. You go in other man world, he have upper hand. He come in you world, you have upper hand. I give example. Many year ago I at Ray Cannon apartment. Ray and me watch Wide World Sport. Muhammed Ali fight pro football player want be boxer. Ali be old. Career over. Pro football man be in good shape. Fight be joke. We watch anyway.

"Football man got no business in ring," say Ray. "Ali old, he still hurt football man."

Ray be right. Football man think he know box. He lift weight. He run. He spar. Ali jab football player anytime he want. Football man keep walking in Ali left hand. Face get bloody. Ali don't use right hand one time.

"Tucker," say Ray, "remember stay in own world. Pro football man don't be boxer. Boxer don't be pro football man."

I be in car man world. Hurley know car. Hurley know how sell car. Car lot be Hurley ring. Hurley smile like he know me whole life. Hurley eye want figure me out. Hurley be sell man. He smell deal, he give time. He don't smell deal, he don't waste time.

Car I want be black limousine. It sit on lot three maybe four week. Hurley know I want car. He read me like I little child book.

He say, "We take ride, Ok?"

Ride be what I think. Hurley talk about how good car be. He say tire be new. He say engine be like forty year old hooker. Plenty mile, still run good put key in.

"How she drive?" he ask.

"Ok," I says.

"What you does?" he ask.

"I parks car, Georgellen Club."

Right there Hurley go quiet.

I brings fighter world everywhere I go. It way I sees thing. Life throw punch. Man get out of way. Sometime man get hit. Man shake off punch. Man punch back. Buy car be two round fight. Hurley win first round. Second round, I change.

"What you want this car?" I asks.

We back at lot. Hurley be at desk. Sonny stand by window, look out at lot. I sits in chair look Hurley in eye.

"Do it matter?" ask Hurley.

"What you means?" I ask.

"Well", say Hurley, "You minds I be honest?"

"No," I says.

"I can't sells you car."

"Why not?" I asks.

"No bank finance you. I don't finance you either. You don't be able afford car."

"How much you want for car?" I asks.

I know what Hurley up to. He know I cash man. He feel me out how much cash I has. Man in this neighborhood go bank, get finance, go better car lot than this.

" Fifteen K," say Hurley.

"Fifteen thousand dollar this car?"

"That right. Sonny, how much this car be worth?" ask Hurley.

"Every penny fifteen K," say Sonny. He still at window.

" Car be worth ten," I says.

"Say who?"

"Say blue book", I says. *Thank you, Kay Jackson,* I thinks. Second round be going good. Too bad Ray Cannon not here.

Night I fight Puerto Rico boy in Buffalo I see thing his face. Ray be right. I win fight, start bad habit that night. Ray Cannon don't know what Tucker Kellogg *see* that night. Puerto Rico boy come at me early. He dance. He move. He hit me everything he have early. He hit me body. He hit me shoulder. He land pretty good punch my forehead. No punch Puerto Rico boy throw hurt Tucker Kellogg. I knows that. Puerto Rico boy know that. Puerto Rico boy face change. Face say, " Oh shit. I don't be able hurt this boy."

Money belt have thirteen thousand dollar. I save thirteen

thousand dollar ten year. No bank. Bank be safe in my closet. Be bolted to floor.

"I give you twelve thousand dollar," I say. "I pay cash. I take car way it be. Car break down, my problem. You write that on paper. I sign."

Me and Hurley does bidness. I takes money belt from jacket. Hurley eye get big. I counts twelve thousand dollar. Money be in ten, twenty, fifty dollar bill. Sonny go get paper work. He fill out title make me owner. He put title in my hand. I put money in Hurley hand. Hurley hand look like it shake a little.

I takes car to Horace Gunn. Horace now call hisself "Bull." I know Horace since we boys in Houston. I tells Horace my plan buy limo. He say he fix anything wrong five hundred dollar, no more. That because we friend long time. Horace look at my car two day. He say car in pretty good shape. He put new belt in car. He put new brake in car. He change oil, flush radiate. He charge three hundred fifty dollar. Horace say engine be used plenty but it have good mile left. Say I take care of car, it get five, maybe ten more year. I tells Horace engine like forty-year-old hooker. Horace don't laugh. He turn queer in prison. Horace be top lady hound we boys. He say one night in prison he hear voice say he gay. Voice say women be reason all trouble his life. Right then he break with womens. That okay with me. He friend.

I get car back second day. I parks car under awning by my building. Car space be assigned. I don't have personal car over year. I walks or rides bus everywhere I goes on island. I leave island, go Houston or other place, I rents car.

I takes night off park car Georgellen Club. I miss two night work, fifteen year. Day mamma die, I miss work. That how important park car be to me. I be real excited about new car. I gets all worked up, can't stay focus. Mind be racing all I wants to do with life. I calms down, be back work tomorrow.

Many thing happen fast. Kay come into my life. Now car come into my life. Dream overload be play my mind. Four week ago, life be dark. Grey sky all time. Now sun shine. Life be bathe in light.

I sits down kitchen my place. Kay be at work. I shows limo to Kay in afternoon. She get real excited. She start planning out loud. She talk about start cook school. She want her and me make lot of money, starts our own bidness.

"Oh, Oh," she say. "I gets ahead my self."

"That OK," I says. "You reason I buys car."

Plan be go slow. Get chauffer license. Get advertise going. Do thing right. I talks Tom York two week ago. He owner of Georgellen Club. Mr. York be bald as egg. He have long arm. Remind me octopus. People say Tom York tell you thing straight. He expect you tell him thing straight. I don't want quits Georgellen Club. I want Georgellen Club job go side by side limo bidness. I tells him I wants keep job park car. He say I be best worker Georgellen Club ever. He say he glad see peoples start own business do good. Self make man be his favorite man. I needs miss work, drives people in limo, he say OK, call in. He say he know rich people in Houston go airport, throw party, always needs limo. I be ready, he put me in touch those peoples. Mr. York serious man. He say "Tucker, you remember man who start Georgellen Club?"

I say, "Yes. Mr. Jax be man who hire me."

Mr. York say "He very good man. He spend life build good thing. I repects good people build good thing. How you sees life?" he ask.

Question catch me off balance. Like weight shift wrong foot. Two thing I knows important man ask you question. *Second* thing be you answer question. *First* thing be you thinks before you answer question.

"Life be ring," I says. "Man get ready for fight, chance of win go up. Man don't get ready for fight, chance of win go down. Win fight, feel good. Lose fight, feel bad. How you sees life?"

Word come out of my mouth surprise me. Tucker Kellogg don't be philosophy man.

"Tucker", say Mr. York "man be born, he be baby. He get on convey belt. Belt run eighty year. Sometime be more, sometime be short. Man die, fall off convey belt. Same convey belt everybody ride. How you act on convey belt say who you be."

* * *

Kitchen be empty, quiet. I closes eyes take slow deep breath. Air go in lung. I holds air. I lets air tell me when let go. Breathe deep, mind focus good. Breathe slow, mind calm down. Breathe in ring, relax, throw good punch. Plenty people in world work hard have nothing show for work. Plenty people in world got nobody. Spend whole life live inside of own head. Tucker Kellogg be lucky. Tucker Kellogg got job, he got woman, he got plan. Tucker Kellogg plan change. Plan get bigger. Plan be own limo bidness, help people close to Tucker Kellogg. Five year from now I have two, maybe three limo car. Ray Cannon need work, he drive for Tucker Kellogg. Howard need job help him go college, he drive for Tucker Kellogg. Thurston show up, need job, he be clean from drug, don't do no crime, he drive for Tucker Kellogg. We be like family. We takes care each other.

I gets up from chair puts on jacket and shoes. I be acting like small boy with new toy. Down stair I go. Lobby door lead to outside. I crosses courtyard near pool. Laundry room be next, then mailbox, then breezeway that open into parking lot.

Five year ago I jump in cab. Be rain cat and dog. Driver and me talk about one night he pick up Diana Ross Supreme. She do concert in Houston. He drive taxi cab then, not limousine. He say own three, four limo, man make money. Light go on Tucker Kellogg head. All time fifteen year park car. Drive, park. Way make money be right under nose. Tucker Kellogg save money hold on dream. Tucker Kellogg know it take more than money.

Take confident. Take hope. Take believe in future.

I turns corner, step in alley. Cars stretch right left under tin awning. Car pull out from park space. Far down, other car turn off headlights. I takes couple of step. Punch I takes in Mobile, end career, don't hurt this bad.

* * *

People has good and bad in them. That be why life be hard. Everybody go around fight little war inside. Best thing do look for good in peoples. Be like hunt for diamond in cave. Couple of week, I be looking for good in me.

I have car three day. Twenty-four hour you count two day Horace Gunn have it. How man suppose believe in God? I kill anybody my life? I sell drug anybody my life? I don't throw one dirty punch whole career. Where it get me?

Like fool, I calls police. Police say car be gone. No point look for car. Car be in Mexico. Car be chop shop, pieces sold. Police take description car, say they be on look out.

"Why anybody want old limo?" I asks.

"Don't know," say police.

"All kind nice car be park close my car," I say.

"Criminal mind pretty smart some people," say police. "Other people mind be like rat. Make no sense what they do. You put two piece cheese out, one be good cheese, other cheese not as good, you think rat say 'This cheese be good, but look here, this cheese be better?' Rat don't think good cheese bad cheese. Cheese be cheese for rat. You has insurance?"

"No," I says.

"Why not?" ask police.

"I has car three day. I plan get insurance."

"I sorry hear this," say police.

Morning after car be stole I tells Kay. Kay be sad. She say, "Tucker, oh no! That a shame. I be sorry." I hear hurt in Kay voice for me. She mean it.

Make angry go away, I goes store, buy bottle Jack Daniel. I has a drink. Drink follow drink. I gets damn stink drunk. Truth, I be drunk one other time my life. I lose fight in Dallas. I think I win fight. Ray Cannon think I win fight. Mr. Jack think I win fight. Crowd think I win fight. I punish other fighter fifteen round. Fight over, I be ready go fifteen more round. Other man have one good round. Hit me two, three time thirteen round. I come back last two round. Punish him again. After fight Mr. Jake say we treat fight like win. Say I do everything right. Ask me I want hooker just like I win. I say "Don't want no woman. Want get drunk." Get drunk don't get rid of worry. Worry be like fly in brain. Fly keep move, don't settle down. Drunk make brain go numb. Like trap fly in block of ice. Fly be there, can't move. Ice melt, fly be there. Fly never go away. Get warm, fly again.

I goes over Kay apartment. Kay let me in. Thing go bad to worse. Howard look at me. His eyes be big. He stand close his mamma.

"You be drunk," say Kay.

"I have drink. I don't be drunk," I say.

"You be drunk. I smells you."

"Why you yell at me? I has bad day. Lose car. Dream be over. I don't comes here yell at you."

"You fools me," she say. "You don't be man you pretends. You be like Howard daddy. He be loser man."

"I don't be loser. I works hard whole life."

Then I hits her. It happen fast. One minute I be in Kay living room, next minute I be in ring. Mind be doing summersault. Punch be left jab. Not hard jab. Catch Kay on side of nose. Electric bolt go through me, say, "What I do?" She bleed all over her blouse. Kay be strong woman. She try hold back tear. Tear come anyway. I don't believe what I do. Tucker Kellogg never hit woman. Never hit anybody outside ring.

Howard look me crazy eyes. Feels like I be outside my body watch me stand in Kay living room. Who that man in Kay living room?

* * *

I hates myself lose Kay. Kay and me don't talk long time. I calls her, try make apologize. She say she know I good man but she be done with me. How Howard know treat women he see his mamma get treat like that? How she trust me not come home like that again? She say her and Howard be ready move away. Howard need man be good example all time. Too much worry she take me back. Howard think she be woman let herself get abuse. Howard see that from his daddy he little boy. World got plenty men choose from treat her better than me. And she don't find man? That be okay too. You gives her choice, take bad man or no man, she take no man any day.

I tries put Kay out my mind. Very hard do. I start go see Mr. Jake in rest house. He be full dementia now. He don't go gym like before.

Ray Cannon go see Mr. Jake every day two, three hour. Ray drop in different time each time he visit. Ray say you drop in same time, staff learn you time come. You drop in different time, staff don't know you come, take better care Mr. Jake.

Monday I sits in with Mr. Jake. Monday be my day off at Georgellen Club. Mr. Jake still have temper. Not easy man spend time with.

Who you think I runs into rest house? You say Kay Jackson, you be right. Kay got new man. Carl be his name. Carl mamma be in rest house too.

Kay and Howard and Carl be family. Howard ask me I still box.

I say "Sure, box be in my blood." I ask, "You still box?"

Howard say, "No."

Kay say, " Howard learn work on car engine with Carl."

Carl introduce self. He be nice fellow. He have strong hand shake. He be like Horace Gunn. Carl look at Kay special way. That be good with me. I be glad Kay and Howard find somebody.

Kay tell me she and Howard live in Houston. She and Carl get married soon. They visit Carl mamma on weekend. Carl mamma have full mind. She move Houston soon be in rest house there. Kay tell Carl and Howard, "Let me speak Tucker for minute"

Carl be good with that. He say nice meet me, give me look. Kay his woman. That door be shut.

"How you do Tucker?" ask Kay.

"I be good," I say. "How you be?"

"Thing be go good," say Kay. "You be see anybody?"

"No," I say. "I don't be good at that"

I look Kay eye. Eye say she happy.

"Kay," I say "one thing I have tell you. I be serious man. I don't be no fool. Man hit you not Tucker Kellogg."

"I knows that," say Kay.

Kay shake my hand. She wish me good. I wish her good thing too. Heart weigh heavy I watch Kay walk out building smile at Carl.

* * *

I works at Georgellen Club. I parks cars. It be first job I has after box. Twenty year go by fast. You ask me twenty year ago I be here this long, I say you some kind of fool.

I comes home park car Georgellen Club, eighty dollar my pocket. I pulls off my trouser, hangs up my jacket. I throws my shirt into clothes hamper. I takes eighty dollar my pocket sets it on dresser with my wallet and keys. I opens safe, floor of my closet. I adds eighty dollars to money be in safe. I closes safe, covers it with pile of old sheet.

Last night I has dream car be mine again. Pair headlight hit wall over my bed make me jump up look out window. I puts dream out my mind. Only one kind dream. That be dream good thing come. No other dream be welcome my head.

I goes out in kitchen opens ice box. I makes corn beef sandwich with pickle. I pours glass cold milk, turns on TV.

ESPN show pair heavyweight. One be black boy rubber skin. He have good right hand. Remember me somebody I know.

All fighter get hit. Good fighter take hit, keep coming. Trade two punch for one. I be in ring, I takes more hit than I gives out. But I always keeps coming. Life be wunaful. Life be wunaful.

The Cop

I got some bad news yesterday. A young doctor confirmed for me what an old doctor told me two days ago: that I had pancreatic cancer and less than a year to live. So I took stock of things. I decided I wouldn't panic or get depressed. I would live every day forward just like I had lived my previous sixty-four years. I wouldn't let death frighten me into major regrets or changes that I had heretofore overlooked. However, one issue trumped everything. I had a life insurance policy worth one hundred thousand dollars. I had nobody to leave the money to and I killed a man thirty years ago.

I was having a lousy day when I answered a call to the scene of a minor traffic accident in my sector. My partner was on sick leave, so it was just me. I'd gotten word from my sergeant an hour earlier, at the front end of my shift, that I passed the exam that would have promoted me from a patrolman to a homicide detective. He also told me that I was being passed over for the promotion in favor of a younger guy who had been on the job just a few years. Our scores were close, but he got the job. I thought the other guy was a good cop but in my view I'd paid my dues. I'd been on the force for thirteen years. I'd picked up a pair of commendations. He was a college graduate with a degree in criminal justice. That, my sergeant confirmed, was the difference maker. He encouraged me not to give up, but I knew I'd never make detective. The people who make those decisions pegged me as a street cop. Or at least I had it that way in my head. Maybe I could've gone back to school and gotten a degree. Or maybe I could've tried the following year, but when I left the station that morning I had a chip on my shoulder.

I wasn't on the road ten minutes when I got the call from dispatch. The accident was within a mile, and I could've driven up on it calmly. It was not a life threatening accident and I knew it. But I was thinking like an angry prick, so I threw on my siren and blew through a red light just to let Greater Houston know that HPD had picked the wrong day to mess with patrolman Gary Francese. And that's how I killed Ian Silver.

When I hit the Chevy Nova that Silver was driving, he was married and the father of two. He was about my age and on his way to work as a draftsman. I hit him broadside on the driver's side. He was the only one in the car. He died immediately. It happened fast. Just before impact he turned and looked me directly in the eyes. I've seen men die. Ian Silver was peaceful. I'll never forget that look.

I myself was injured. I broke my left leg below the knee. I spent a few days in the hospital then went on sick leave for nine weeks. I wore a cast. When I came back to work I stayed inside doing light duty until my supervisor and a psychologist were convinced I was ready to go back on patrol.

Needless to say, both the City and I got sued. I saw it coming because I had it coming. Ian Silver was in the prime of his life. His widow sued for wrongful death. Her loss of spousal consortium coupled with his lost income projected over a working life of thirty-five years resulted in a request for a million dollars from the City and me jointly and severally. If I sound like a lawyer it's because I paid very close attention to my attorney.

But Mrs. Silver settled for peanuts. She let it all go for fifty thousand dollars. And to this day I don't know why. The City's insurance carrier paid the bill and we all moved on in life. I was curious for a while but didn't push it. Both the City and I got the same letter from our attorney stating that the matter was over and that an out of court settlement had been reached. I never mentioned the suit again. It never passed my lips. My mother raised no fool.

The following year I didn't reapply for the detective job. Two more positions had opened up, one due to a retirement and the other a result of an expanded city budget. I wasn't interested. My desk sergeant pushed me to try again, but now I had a soiled history with people who never saw me as detective material in the first place. The guilt I felt over Ian Silver's death made me less than deserving. I resigned myself to the role of street cop.

Slowly but surely a damaged psychology controlled my life. The guilt and the depression never went away fully. Over the next thirty years I was married twice. Both marriages resulted in divorce. I drank, sometimes heavily. I jumped on and off the wagon. I joined AA. I'd stay sober for a year or two at a time then I'd drink hard. On my days off I was miserable to be around. I was a mean drunk who drove both women away.

Finally, I retired. I said goodbye to the police force. By the time I left there was nobody around who I related to any more. Everybody was young. Most of the new cops were college educated, or ex-military and tech savvy. I didn't fit in. The game had passed me by.

What little peace I got as a cop came from fishing. After my second divorce I spent most of my free time catching fish up and down the Gulf Coast. I found myself spending more and more time on Galveston Island. I decided to retire there and took up residence in a retirement village on the Island.

I continued drinking. I dropped AA. I wasn't interested in sobriety. I enjoyed getting drunk. Who was I hurting? I had a car but I rarely left the Island. I walked everywhere. When I drank with the intention of getting drunk I stayed in my apartment. I met a few women in the village but never let anything get started. I figured they'd try to get me to stop drinking and I wasn't going to do that. With a woman, if you're not willing to change, it's a dead end you don't need to go down.

I woke up one morning with indigestion. I figured it for some red snapper I had the night before. It had a funny taste from what I thought was freezer burn. I give away a lot of the fish I catch. The rest I wrap up in plastic bags or aluminum foil then stow it away in the freezer compartment of my icebox. With all the fishing I do I've got a constant supply of red fish, bonita, and flounder. It's good eating but every now and then you get a bad fish or the frost ruins it. In any case, I let it go. Then it became chronic. I'd get a queasy stomach sometimes that would stay for days. So, I stopped eating. I lost my appetite and along with it my weight. I dropped twenty pounds fast. I was always a little on the chubby side so at first people told me I looked good with the lost pounds. I kept hoping the bad stomach would go away. I thought I might have an ulcer. I put off going to a doctor. I don't like doctors. They scare me. Things got worse. My guts started hurting and I felt bloated despite not eating enough to keep a bird alive. My eyes turned yellow. I knew something serious was going on.

I finally saw a doctor on the Island. He was an older man I trusted. I won't go to a woman doctor. If I get naked in front of a female it's for the purpose of adult recreation. The words "pancreatic cancer" came out of his mouth. I pushed him for more, but he told me to get into a specialist he recommended as soon as possible. I did what he told me. We made the appointment right then and there from his office. I was in Houston the next morning for an internist. He was a young guy, all business, who ran some tests then got back to me two days later confirming the first diagnosis. I asked him what I could do.

Were there treatments? I'd stop drinking. I'd exercise. I was already a healthy eater what with all the fish I caught.

"I wish I could give you better news," he said. "But this stuff has spread all over. Unfortunately, the way it works with pancreatic cancer, you don't feel the symptoms until it's too late."

"And it's too late?" I asked.

"I'm afraid so, Mr. Francese, short of a bona fide miracle."

So I was a dead man - a dead man with, however, time to reflect. Ian Silver's face, always with me, but never as clear as it was now, with it's peaceful look, reminded me that if nothing else I could make things right. I decided to look up Donna Silver.

When she lost her husband, Donna Silver was twenty-five years old. I know that much about her, but nothing more. Whereas Ian Silver's face is stamped permanently in my brain, I have trouble remembering his widow at all. Maybe it's because I couldn't look her in the eye during the deposition which was the only time she and I were in the same room. She was young and a little plump, what you'd think a young mother of two would look like. She could come up to me now and I wouldn't know her. As for the two kids, there was a boy and a girl, both of them under ten. I've never met or seen either of them.

If I was going to find the Silver family, or what was left of it, I needed a place to start. I had a copy of the lawsuit that named the attorney, Blake Rousseau, who had represented me and the City. It was easy enough to call the City attorney's office but nobody there was much help. A secretary with a good memory recalled that he left public practice for a job out of state. I called the State Bar. That went nowhere. I became impatient which reminded me why I never made the rank of detective. I looked in the Houston phone book on the off chance he or anyone named Silver might be in there. Nothing came of that. Finally, I called August Spivey. August was a private eye, a straight shooter who I could trust to do good work and keep things confidential. He and I met in the Georgellen Club, the both of us drinking the stuff that no doubt played a big role in killing me.

"Pay me my expenses," said Spivey. "If I turn up anything, I'll add $250 on top of that."

"I can pay more," I said. "This is important to me."

"I'm charging you what I normally charge for a locate job. No more, no less" said Spivey.

"Do you think you'll find them?" I asked.

"If they're around, I'll find them," assured Spivey.

We left it at that. It was pure handshake. I knew him and his brother, Jack, an attorney, to be honorable types. Spivey reported in every other day with a synopsis of what he did, how much time he put in, and how much my bill was running. After six days, he called me.

"The mother's dead" he said. "So's the son. But Ian Silver's daughter is a lawyer name of Gloria Loper. She's in Houston. Looks like she might be a big time lawyer. The downtown variety."

Spivey gave me the name of her firm that was, in fact, one of the heavy hitters in Houston's legal community. Spivey followed with his bill that totaled $600. I threw in an extra $100 as a tip. I didn't ask him how he found Gloria Loper or how he knew that her mother and brother were dead. For all I knew, he might have gone to their old neighborhood and knocked on doors until he found some people who remembered the family. It made me no matter. I thought about whether I really wanted to face the daughter of the man I killed because I was angry over a lost promotion. It was something I needed to do.

I drove to Houston two Mondays later. I called ahead and made an appointment to see Gloria Loper but was rebuffed by a secretary who put me through the standard questions about who I was and what I needed Mrs. Loper for. I told her my name and that I might have an insurance settlement for Mrs. Loper. An hour later I got a call from that same secretary setting the appointment.

The morning of the meeting I got up, showered, and tried to eat but nothing was staying down. I-45 into downtown Houston is busy during rush hour so I got an early start figuring two hours at a minimum. I pulled into the parking garage of Booker, Best, and Cody at quarter to nine. I had this horrible image of the Silver kids growing up without any chance for success because of me, but Ian Silver's daughter turned out pretty well.

She was a tall woman, thin, stately, red haired. She had the build of a model, not a beautiful woman facially but enough going on downstairs to make up for any lack of natural beauty. And her face. It was Ian Silver's face. I was looking into the face of Ian Silver.

"I don't need your money, Mr. Francese, but thanks."

"It would help me if you'd take it," I said.

"I'm not interested in helping you," she said.

"Your life, was it hard after your father died?"

"Yes," she said, "very much so."

"I suppose your family hated me," I stated.

"We did, but that doesn't buy groceries. We got on with our lives."

She studied me. She had a piercing somewhat predatory look. She was all lawyer. I assumed she was married by virtue of her last name but I didn't ask. My gut feeling was that she loved the people close to her and was all business with everyone else.

"It's a lot of money," I said. "I'd sure like you to have it."

"You've given me what I needed, Mr. Francese. I always wanted to meet the man who killed my father. I figured you for a much taller man. We're done here. "

I nodded and left. A couple of weeks went by. I felt myself grow weaker. It was becoming clear that the year my doctors gave me was a best case scenario. I wasn't going to live much longer. I didn't want to. I had no heart for life. The tedium was coming to an end.

I went to see my insurance agent to change beneficiaries in my policy. The fellow who sold it to me was long gone like I would soon be. I sat down with a young woman, not too far removed from her college days, and changed my beneficiary from my last ex wife (God knows where she was or even if she was alive) over to the Sisters of the Holy Spirit. They were the nuns who taught me good from bad. I couldn't think of a better bunch to substitute in lieu of Ian Silver's daughter.

We did the paperwork and I left the building. As I turned a corner in downtown Houston, my car parked in the law firm's lot several blocks away, I saw a familiar face. It was Blake Rousseau. He was thirty years older, but as fit and tan and relaxed as I had always hoped I would be. You don't look that good from grinding away at work sixty hours a week. He was retired, living in South Carolina, this week in Houston for his niece's wedding. He didn't recognize me at first, but with some prodding and an apology from me for stopping him on the street, was amiable and in no particular hurry to rush off. So it is with the happily retired.

"But why," I asked, "would Mrs. Silver have settled for such a small amount of money?"

"Well, for one thing," said Rousseau, "her husband had no insurance and she was strapped for cash as it was. So we, I mean you and the City, were in a stronger position."

"So she could've used the million dollars?" I asked. "Correct?"

"Well sure," said Rousseau, "who couldn't use a million bucks? But she had no leverage. She was lucky she got what we offered. It didn't hurt either that she had a lawyer who was afraid to go to trial. I smelled that early."

"So, why did she settle?" I asked.

"Well, the City and you were liable, but when we broke down the case and threatened to take it to trial on the issue of damages, she had nothing. Look I have to run."

"But why? Why didn't she have any damages?" I asked.

Rousseau strolled away, looking over his shoulder.

"We got hold of Ian Silver's medical records. He was a dead man. He was dying of pancreatic cancer."

The Lawyer

I stopped drinking a year ago. I was fifty-two and, since I come from a family of alcoholics, thought it a good idea. My father was an alcoholic, my brother is an alcoholic, and yes, I, too, pay homage to the bottle.

When I drank, I drank at the Georgellen Club. I am not a fellow who likes to drink alone. I cannot sit in my kitchen pouring one shot after another. I need people when I drink, people I can talk to, people who will listen to my stories.

I have tried other bars. I have no complaints about them. The people were friendly. And, generally speaking, a drunk is a drunk no matter where you go.

I like the Georgellen Club because its patrons, me included, have something missing. If I'm wrong, I drink in the wrong bar.

I tend to get friendly with bartenders. There have been quite a few. Two in particular come to mind.

One is Andy Rogers, a thin, red haired man with a hard look. I have been told, by sources unreliable, that he is skillful with a knife.

The other is Billy Brown. Billy is that boy you turned to

when your regular friends were unavailable. You walked outside one day, bored, looking for something to do, and there was Billy, across the street, shooting baskets by himself. You always had a good time with Billy because he was so glad to see you. But when your regular friends came around, Billy went back to being alone. Did I know this for a fact about him? No, I sensed this for I can spot the lonely.

Billy Brown had a good-looking wife, the kind that male fantasies are made of. How a woman who looked like that connected with an uninteresting fellow like Billy Brown baffled me unless, perhaps, she had spotted in Billy the same utility that I had.

In retrospect, as an insight into the strange dynamic between Billy and Esther Brown, I did not know for several weeks that they had been married despite the fact that Esther came into the Georgellen Club regularly and sat at the bar. I was there.

She ordered her drinks from Billy but directed virtually all of her attention and conversation toward Andy Rogers. Billy Brown may as well have never existed. And it was only when I mentioned indiscreetly to the fellow seated next to me at the bar, that Andy's girlfriend looked truly fuckable that Billy overheard me and told me that she had been his wife.

I apologized sincerely for my crude remark and asked if he wanted me to leave. He shrugged and told me "no." That remark, for which I was deeply embarrassed despite his apparent forgiveness coupled with my own musings about sobriety, awakened in me a desire to change. I resolved that night to quit drinking. I finished the drink in hand, pronounced to myself that I was through, paid my bar bill, and left.

As I exited the club, my life in review, I wondered if I had become the man I wanted to be. Had I expected this? Seen it coming? There I was, a fifty-two year old drunk, yes, a drunk, with no one, who looked at other men's wives and then, on the sly, slipped in an occasional lasciviousness just to convince myself I was one of the boys.

That night, as I walked across the parking lot of the club, several strides from my car, I heard footsteps. They came from behind, soft, almost swishing over the asphalt. I turned, frightened at the prospect of encountering a mugger.

"Hey, can we talk?" It was Billy Brown.

"Yes," I answered with false calmness.

"Are you a lawyer?"

"I am."

"I didn't know that until a minute ago."

"I don't tell people."

"What kind of lawyer?"

"Real estate."

"You wouldn't want to help a guy, would you?"

The journey that had brought me to that point in the parking lot of the Georgellen Club had been, for the most part, marked by accident and minimal resistance. I was, in the parlance of my profession, a dirt lawyer. I practiced real estate law for a bank.

"How so?" I asked stiffly.

"Have you got a minute?"

"I do."

The marriage of Billy Brown, the condensed version, went something like this. He and Esther met twelve years ago. He was thirty-six. She was eighteen. I thought, certainly, that he would tell me he had been an athlete for he possessed the thick body and short hair of one, or perhaps a former roughneck from the oil fields but no, he was then, as he was now, a bartender.

Esther Brown had been Esther Kaulhaus, which sounded German, but I did not ask. Billy Brown was an open book, telling me things about him and Esther that I neither wanted nor needed to know. Esther, at eighteen, had wanted out of a rather dreary life. She had grown up in South Texas, and had, after leaving high school in the eleventh grade, worked an assortment of menial jobs the last of which was cleaning rooms in a Holiday Inn.

It was there she met Billy Brown and it was there, in Billy's room, they conceived Natalie. "Would you like to see Natalie?" he asked.

"Sure," I shrugged.

From his pocket he produced a brown wallet within which was a series of credit cards and pictures. From those he culled Natalie, a marginally cute, thick child with honey blond hair who would never look like her mother. I nodded then commented how much daughter resembled father.

That the marriage had lasted as long as it had was, to me, remarkable, for Billy Brown seemed not the caliber of man who could keep the likes of Esther, to any degree, happy. Nor did Esther impress me as possessing even a scintilla of selflessness, a trait I associate with successful marriages. I base this solely upon my observations of her in the club. I did not know her, nor did I ever see her with her daughter. She may have been a loving mother. But to Billy Brown, from where I stood, she was worthless baggage, the kind he needed to discard.

So there, in the parking lot of the Georgellen Club, near my car, a bit drunk, I listened as Billy Brown recounted stories of Esther's infidelities, of drunkenness and wantonness beyond shame, and of their recent divorce.

"You're already divorced?" I asked.

"Yeah."

"But she's in the bar right now."

"I know that."

"Doesn't that seem a bit odd to you, you, bartending, her, your ex-wife, drinking and picking up men not six feet away?"

"No."

I know my look was puzzled. Perhaps that prompted Billy Brown to continue.

"I don't care a damn about Esther. I did once, but now she's free to fuck anybody she wants. I'm concerned about my daughter."

"And where is your daughter now?"

"At home, I guess, with a sitter."

"You don't know?"

"Nope."

"Why not?"

"I can't go near the house."

"Go on," I said.

"I popped Esther."

"But she's in the bar."

"Didn't I just say that I knew that? I can't go near the house. Besides, she's not afraid of me. She knows I won't hit her again. I smacked her once. She was fooling around with a strange guy in our kitchen. Who wouldn't get a little crazy?"

I found the relative calm with which Billy Brown expressed his sordid life alluring, even to the point of myself feeling a bit charmed. It was neither the voice of resignation nor indifference but that of someone with rather thick skin. I did, however, hear in that voice authentic concern for his daughter.

"I just want to get Natalie away from her. I'm desperate."

"And you want me to help you get full custody of her," I stated.

"Yes, I do."

"But you, sir, need a trial lawyer."

The puzzled look now belonged to him.

"Let me explain," I continued. "You are a bartender, are you not?"

"I am."

"And you mix drinks?"

"Yes."

"All sorts of drinks?"

" My share."

"How many would you say you couldn't mix?"

"I don't know. A dozen."

"And if someone came along, and asked you to provide your services at a party, a special party, a wedding for instance, wherein those drinks you can't mix were to be served, what would you do?"

"Learn how to mix them."

"Yes, but what if there was a possibility, remote as it might be, that, on short notice, you might not learn how to mix those drinks? Would you then expect those people to hire you?"

"If they had no choice, yeah," he answered.

I waited for Billy Brown to see the light, to understand that I was not the man for the job. He stood there, as did I, silently, waiting, I suppose, for me to take it. Something told me, were he in my shoes, he would.

"I can't."

"Why not?" he asked.

"Because I don't have it in me," I admitted.

The next morning, I went to work. The night before I had seen Billy Brown, his head bowed, walk off into the dark. I did not feel like much of a man. I visited the office of a fellow attorney, Gus Farrow, who confirmed for me that he too would have rejected such a proposal.

That weekend I wanted desperately to visit the club, to drink, to tell my stories. There were things I simply could not let go of. What if this young girl grew up to be every bit as lost and confused as her mother? What if her mother who, for all I knew, really loved her daughter and was not the terrible woman Billy Brown had described? What of Billy Brown? Did I not feel at least some guilt about the way I treated, not only him, but those like him? And what about me who had made, in my fifty-two years, absolutely no difference in the life of another?

I called him on Sunday. I looked through the phone book, found several names that could have been his, and then dialed.

After three attempts we connected.

I met Billy Brown at his apartment. He lived as I thought he would—spare, with blank white walls, a television, and a couch. He asked me what changed my mind. I told him the State Bar expected a certain level of pro bono work from its attorneys. Not knowing what pro bono meant, he asked me to explain. I replied "Pro Bono Publico -- For the good of the public."

I made it clear to him that I was not a litigator and that I had never been in a trial. I brought people together over land deals. This could quite easily fall apart. I wanted him to understand what he was getting into.

But I saw that I could do no wrong with Billy Brown. Had he been a dog he would have licked my hand. We conversed there, on his couch, a bit about strategy. I would draft a petition, the purpose of which was to modify custody, and an order that, should we prevail, would be presented to the presiding judge for signature.

I would also, by letter, suggest to Esther Brown, that, in my view, her best choice, what with the body of evidence we would assemble, all of it clearly and convincingly proving her unfit as a mother, was to gracefully and maturely give up custody of Natalie.

There was, however, the matter of counsel. Would Esther Brown have an attorney? Billy Brown said she had no means with which to hire one. I reminded myself, and informed him, of Legal Aid, that she might very well have an attorney, adequate at least, and certainly more experienced at trial than me. Nevertheless, I went forward. In this matter, I felt on the side of good.

For the next three weeks I educated myself in Family Law. During the day I worked at my job and at night, usually until one or so in the morning, I poured over new material.

I found myself changing. I was never, for instance, at my own job more competent. I had no time to nurture my insecurities. I became somewhat gruff, yet swiftly came to the point, telling the other attorneys to take my employer's deal or leave it. They, and their clients, fell into line without as much as a snort.

At my direction, Billy Brown assembled our evidence. There was a police report wherein Esther had been beaten by a live-in boyfriend. Drugs were found on the premises. There was another police report of driving while intoxicated. There were attendance records from two different schools both evidencing Natalie's excessive truancy, all of this occurring under Esther's watch.

And then there was Natalie.

I thought it prudent to meet the little girl who was at the center of this storm. I did not know how we would do it. Esther was, according to Billy, rather haphazard about visitation, following the divorce order when it suited her. She was prone, on some Sundays when Billy was off from work, to dropping her daughter, without warning, at his doorstep. Billy accepted this without complaint, always glad to see Natalie.

On one such Sunday he phoned me. Without hesitation I made the drive over. Natalie, in my view mature for her years, extended her hand politely. Daughter, father and I sat for a while chatting pleasantly until Billy Brown announced that he needed to run an errand. Natalie and I visited alone.

"Well, Natalie," I began, "has your father told you what this is about?"

"Yes," she nodded.

"Is it a hard thing or an easy thing?"

She shrugged then said "Hard, but I want to do it."

"Do you love your mother?"

"Yes," she answered.

"Do you love your father?"

"Yes."

"If you had to pick one or the other to live with, who

would it be?"

"My daddy," she answered.

"May I ask why?"

"He's more grown up."

"In what way?" I asked.

"He makes me do my homework and go to bed."

"And your mother doesn't do that?"

"No, sir."

"If she did those things would you want to live with her then?"

"No, sir."

"Why not?"

"Because she gets drunk."

"Do you know what drunk means?" I asked.

"Yes, sir."

"What?"

"She drinks too much beer and whiskey."

"How do you know it's too much?"

"Because she talks funny."

"Does that bother you?"

"Yes, sir."

"Why?"

"Because…I don't know…her boyfriends kiss her all over when she gets that way."

"Does she have boyfriends?"

"Yes, sir."

"How many?"

"Lots."

"Do you know them?"

"No, sir."

"Why not?"

"They don't say their names."

"Are you there when they visit?"

"Yes, sir."

"Where?"

"In the living room."

"Doing what?"

"Watching TV."

"Do they watch TV with you?"

"No, sir."

"What do they do?"

"They go in her room."

If push came to shove, as distasteful as I found it, I would witness Natalie Brown against her mother. Would she do this?

"Natalie, I'm going to ask you a hard question but I need you to tell me the truth."

"Yes, sir."

"If I ask you questions like these, in front of a lot of people, could you answer them just like you did now?"

"Yes, sir."

"If your mother was in the room, would that be hard?"

"Yes, sir."

"But could you do it?"

"Yes, sir."

"Why, Natalie?"

"Because I don't want to be like her."

Billy Brown returned. I said goodbye to Natalie. Billy and I talked for a few minutes, outside, beside my car. I asked him how he felt about Natalie as a witness. If that is what it took, and it was acceptable to Natalie, he was willing.

That evening I drafted a Petition seeking to modify custody and my letter to Esther Brown wherein I identified myself as Billy's attorney. I informed her that, before her reading of the letter, the Petition would be filed with the District Clerk. I also included my draft of a Consent Decree wherein she, without contest, awarded custody of her daughter to Billy Brown.

My letter was not threatening. I encouraged her to seek legal counsel but cautioned her that my client was serious, would not negotiate, and would carry the matter through. I made my trip to the courthouse the following day after work, slipping into the clerk's office just ahead of closing. The following morning I sent the letter with its packet within which were my drafts and a return envelope hoping that Esther would see the light, sign the Consent Decree, and put this thing to rest. I awaited her call, or, perhaps, the call of her attorney.

I was at my desk, pouring over a mortgage, when the call came. I had spoken to two attorneys that morning, one representing the seller, the other, the buyer, in a deal my employer would lend on that afternoon.

Typically, I work with my door open. My fellow attorneys are welcome in my office. That morning, I kept the door closed. My phone rang at 10 AM.

"Is this Jack Spivey?"

"Yes, it is."

"This is Esther Brown. I'm holding your letter."

I expected, especially after hearing her from time to time at the club, an Esther Brown who was at least unsophisticated if not coarse. She surprised me with a demeanor that was initially polite.

"Mrs. Brown," I said, for she had not changed her name, "before we continue, are you represented by an attorney?"

"No, I am not."

"Do you plan on hiring one?"

"I don't know yet."

"Then, let me advise you that I represent your ex-husband in this matter."

"Yes, your letter says that. May I ask you a question?"

"Certainly."

"Is Billy paying you?"

"No, he is not."

I spoke candidly, although I considered that a confidential matter between Billy Brown and me.

"What are you getting for this?"

"Nothing,"

"You're doing this for free?"

"Yes, I am."

"Why?"

"I believe it to be the right thing to do."

Esther Brown sighed.

"Oh Christ. The right thing."

"Yes ma'am. I agree with your ex husband. We think it is in the best interest of your daughter that she lives with her father."

"I know who you are. You're the guy who drinks at the club. I've seen you look at me. Is this some way of trying to meet me?"

"No, Mrs. Brown. I have no desire to meet you."

"Are you even a real lawyer?"

"I can assure you that I am."

"Well let me assure you of something you lonely freak. I won't give up my daughter. Not to that loser of an ex. And if you're the best he can do...."

She left the insult incomplete, choosing instead to hang up the phone. I was disappointed and, yes, somewhat anxious that she had not cooperated. I decided to have her served.

My brother, Augie, is a private investigator. A good one. Among those services he offers is the delivery of civil process. He is well regarded in the legal community for it is rare that he fails to place notice of suit, if not in the hand of the receiving party, then surely at his feet. To the best of my knowledge, and I would have heard about it, not one of his deliveries has been contested in court. He is, however, a man whose appetites generally get the better of him. Two days later, I answered another phone call.

"Jack"

"Yes, Augie."

"I got her served."

"How did it go?"

"I put the paper in her hand."

"Was her daughter there?"

"I don't know. She met me at the door."

"How did she act?"

"Well Jack, she was naked."

"What do you mean?"

"I mean she didn't have anything on."

"At all?"

"She was holding a wash cloth. She invited me in."

I said nothing. Augie knew what that meant.

"Jack, I was strong."

"How strong, Augie?"

"Very strong."

"You know what she was trying to do, don't you?" I asked.

"Discredit the service?"

"Yes, and me and you and this whole case."

"You think she's that smart?"

"I think she understands men."

Two weeks later, as though nothing had happened, Esther dropped her daughter off at Billy Brown's apartment. No mention was made of the lawsuit which, upon reflection, did not surprise me as I considered Esther capable of discretion if it advanced her cause. I was surprised, however, when Billy reported to me that his ex-wife had not picked up Natalie at the agreed time, or any time thereafter. Further, her phone had been disconnected. Upon visiting his former home, a rent house, Billy Brown discovered it vacated. A phone call to the landlord produced no forwarding address.

I considered this good news. Had Esther Brown given up? Would she not show up in court wherein a default judgment would be rendered?

My hackles rose. Esther Brown had twenty days within which to answer our suit. Perhaps she had moved in with a new boyfriend or left the city altogether. I prepared myself, just in case, for trial, reviewing evidence, scripting my direct examination, anticipating my cross, if it came to that, of Esther Brown.

Though I worked diligently at my own job, I kept attention to the calendar, each day placing another checkmark on another day gone by. On day nineteen, Billy Brown phoned me at home.

"Guess what?" he asked.

"What?" I answered.

"Esther showed up last night."

"Where?"

"At the club."

"You were working?"

"Yes, what else would I be doing there?"

"What did she say?"

"She laughed. Then she gave me a piece of paper."

"Do you have it now?" I asked.

"Yes."

"What does it say at the top?"

I heard paper crinkle.

"It says 'Answer.' What does that mean?"

"Remember," I explained, "when I told you that a lawsuit is a little like a football game?"

"Yes," said Billy Brown.

"And that if the other team doesn't show up for kickoff, we win by forfeit?"

"Yes."

"Well," I sighed, "the other team showed up."

I thought for a moment.

"Does it look like Esther wrote it?"

"No," said Billy Brown. "Esther couldn't do something

like this on her own."

"Is there a lawyer's name on the bottom?" I asked.

"No."

"Well, if Esther didn't draft it, I can only conclude that she had a lawyer draft it for her. But no lawyer contacted me. She's not represented. I don't get it."

"I do," said Billy Brown. "Esther's not above fucking another lawyer."

I visited the Clerk of Court where I obtained, upon request, Billy's and Esther Brown's divorce file. In it was a copy of the Answer that Billy had described to me over the phone. Billy was correct. Clearly, Esther had not drafted it. I obtained from the clerk a photocopy, verified the Hearing date, and then jotted down Esther's last known address, a post office box on the Gulf Freeway.

Ninety days had passed since I agreed to represent Billy Brown. As the hearing approached, I grew edgier. I practiced. I scripted. I worried. Two days before the hearing, I answered a knock on my door. It was Billy Brown.

"Look what I have." he said.

In his hand was an executed copy of the Consent Decree I had failed at getting Esther Brown to sign. I gave it a cursory read. It appeared satisfactory.

"How did you get this?"

"I went over to see her."

"How did you find her?"

"Think about it," responded Brown.

I had heretofore not seen him sneer as he did now. I shrugged.

"She was at Andy Roger's."

"You're kidding!"

"No," he said, shaking his head.

"Does that surprise you?" I asked.

"No, should it?"

"Well," I said, "for one, you work with him."

"You've never seen him and Esther in the club?" Brown questioned.

"How did you find out?"

"I took a gamble they'd be shacked up."

"Where was Rogers?"

"Working."

"And you went over there?"

"Yes."

"How did Esther react?"

"Surprised. Then pissed off."

"How did you get her to sign?"

"I brought Natalie along."

"Honestly?"

"Uh huh. And Esther cussed me. But then I reminded her Natalie was going to be a witness."

"But she knew that," I argued. "I sent her a witness list."

"Yeah," agreed Brown, "but that's not how Esther's mind works. You have to put it right in her face."

"Did she say anything to Natalie?" I asked.

"Oh Yeah. 'Please, baby don't do this.' Stuff like that. But Natalie wouldn't buckle. She torqued that little jaw of hers and stood her ground." Billy Brown raised the paper. "So, we're in pretty good shape?" he asked.

The night before the hearing I slept surprisingly well, somehow dismissing the mishmash of law and strategy in my mind that had played over repeatedly for several days. I took Thursday and Friday off from work, thinking that one day might spill over into another.

Billy and I had decided to meet at his place and go from there. I wore a charcoal grey suit, white shirt, and a blue tie along with a pair of wing tips I kept for special occasions. I made it clear to Billy that he needed to dress for court and that meant a suit and a tie but he, having neither, wore dark slacks and a white, long-sleeved shirt open at the collar. Natalie wore a pink dress with white shoes.

We went in Billy's car, he and Natalie in the front, me in the back briefing them as we drove. We would go directly to the Clerk of Court, pick up the file, and then head directly to the assigned courtroom. We would sign the docket sheet, placing our action, hopefully, at or near the front, and then take a seat. If things went well, we might be done that morning.

As we sat, the courtroom filled steadily. I fully expected Esther Brown, accompanied, perhaps, by an attorney plucked from Legal Aid, to show up. But she did not.

Upon the judge's entry from chambers we, on command, stood then reseated ourselves. The judge, a boyish looking fellow with glasses, handled what appeared to be several ministerial acts then began hearing cases. We, as planned, were first on the docket and announced, "ready".

I approached and stood before the bench. Billy Brown and daughter remained in their seats. I handed the file to the judge.

"Your Honor, let me first state that I am a real estate attorney and am representing my client on a pro bono basis."

"Go on,'" he said, opening the file.

"I have with me a Consent Decree whereby Defendant Esther Brown has agreed to relinquish full custody of their daughter, Natalie Brown, to her ex-husband, Plaintiff William Brown."

"Was she served properly?"

"Yes, Your Honor, at all times, at every turn, both by personal service and certified mail."

"And you have affidavits to that effect?"

"From the process server?" I asked.

"Correct," he answered.

"Yes, I do."

I stepped forward and from the file produced Augie's

affidavit. After inspecting it, and the Decree, he rested his chin on folded hands.

"How did you go about getting the Defendant to sign this?"

"Her ex-husband obtained it."

"And were you there?"

"No, Your Honor, I was not."

"Was she represented by counsel?"

"No, Your Honor. However, I was completely forthright with her, gave her no advice, and suggested to her that she hire an attorney."

"Was duress employed in obtaining this?"

"We made it clear, Your Honor, that my client had a wealth of supporting evidence all of which appears in the file before you. And to be fully candid, it was my plan, assuming the Court would allow, to use her daughter as a witness."

"Against her own mother?"

"Yes, Your Honor."

"And the girl was willing?"

"Fully."

He looked at Esther Brown's signature.

"Is this her's?"

"Yes, Your Honor."

"But you didn't see her execute this?"

"No, Your Honor."

"I notice that her signature is not notarized."

"I note that as well Your Honor."

I paused, flustered a bit, and then a light came on.

"Your Honor, if it pleases the Court, Plaintiff Brown is here. He could be sworn in and, under oath, authenticate her signature."

The judge nodded and I summoned Billy Brown forward, pointing at him, but not Natalie. I explained what was to take place then stood aside my client as he raised his hand. At the judge's inquiry, he identified Esther Brown's signature. On command, we stepped back as the judge affixed his name to the Decree.

"Ordered," he pronounced.

So it was done. We returned the file to the Clerk of Court, requesting that she send certified copies both to Billy Brown and Esther at their respective addresses. Upon reaching the parking lot of Billy Brown's apartment he shook my hand warmly.

"I owe you so much," he said.

"You owe me nothing," I stated. I would have, however, accepted a nice lunch at a fine eatery. Steak was on my mind.

"What are you going to do?"

"I don't know," he said. "Rest for a day or two, I guess."

"What's Esther going to do?"

"She told me," remarked Billy Brown, "that she might enlist in the army."

"When did she tell you that?"

"Two nights ago."

"You think she means it?"

"No, that's Esther. She dreams. I don't see her in the US Army."

"I don't either" I agreed, but easily imagined the US Army in Esther.

I shook hands with Natalie Brown, knowing I had done a good thing, and then drove away.

* * *

I started drinking six weeks ago. I missed the warm nurture of alcohol. How it made me feel safe, as though I were nestled in the palm of a large, soft hand. And I missed the club, for truthfully without it I had nothing but my work.

The first night back I nursed my favorite drink, that being as much Scotch as could fit into a small iceless glass. I decided that would do for now. I was, after all, on step one of learning how to drink again.

I noticed that there was no Billy Brown behind the bar. I had neither seen nor heard from him since that day in the parking lot. Andy Rogers was there, sharing duties with another bartender I did not know.

"Haven't seen you in a while," remarked Rogers. "You quit drinking?"

"Yes I did in fact," I said, which seemed to surprise him. "What happened to Billy Brown?"

"He moved to Amarillo."

"When?"

"Six months ago."

"And his ex-wife?"

Rogers smiled.

"She's in Missouri."

"Why there?"

"Her family's there," he answered.

He walked away from me to wait on another customer. A few minutes later he returned.

"Say, are you a lawyer?"

"I am," I responded.

"How come you never said so?"

"I don't want people to know."

"What kind of lawyer are you?"

"Real Estate," I answered.

"You wouldn't want to help a guy out, would you?"

"No," I said definitively.

He left to wait on yet another customer. I finished my drink and, in a gesture intended to smooth things out, left ten dollars in his jar. He saw me do that, nodding slightly. Bartenders are not prone to gushing over tips.

"Say," he said as I turned.

"Yes?"

"Billy's and Esther's girl, Natalie."

"Yes," I acknowledged.

"She's back with Esther."

"How do you know that?"

"Esther called me, wanting money. She and the girl are in Missouri."

That, I could not fathom.

"Do I look stupid?" I inquired.

"No," answered Rogers.

"Are you thinking I'm some sort of chump?"

"No".

"It's okay if you are," I stated, "because I am."

"Don't worry about it," said Rogers. "I should have never brought it up."

"But you did. Why did she leave her father?"

"Hell, that girl's coming into puberty. Esther got into her little head. She's a cat teaching her kitty how to hunt."

Rogers walked away. I was neither angry nor surprised once I considered everything. I had done a good deed. I'd learned a few things. And, for a while, I'd been a better lawyer. Besides, who was I to believe in anyone? It was good to be back at the Georgellen Club.

The Priest

Things began well. I attended Catholic grade school. After the eighth grade, two classmates and I went off to the seminary. (I won't mention the Order, so great was the disservice I did it.) My grade school classmates eventually quit, realizing the priesthood was not for them. I, on the other hand, remained. I finished high school and college as a seminarian. I was ordained a Catholic priest.

God's call, I believed, was a miracle. While in church, as a boy with my parents, listening somewhat indifferently to our pastor eulogize the loss of one of our own, a missionary who had died spreading the gospel in the jungles of Central America, I noticed a tear, red as blood, trickle down the cheek of a women two pews over. This vision would never go away. In fact, it is today, despite everything, etched indelibly in my psyche. Whether real or imaginary, it made no difference to me. It became for me tangible proof of God's choice of me to serve in His holy priesthood.

I came up through the ranks. I loved everything about the priesthood—the sacraments, the power of the pulpit. At age forty, I had my own parish, a beautiful gem in rural Nebraska. It was six hundred families of hard working, God fearing people, salt of the earth souls to shepherd and save. They were my surrogate children. I baptized them. I blessed them. I buried them. And I had a good sense for business. I built a new church, converting the old building into additional classrooms. Our school was top notch. I had ten sisters, living on campus in a nice warm convent, and eight lay teachers, educating grades kindergarten through eighth, two classrooms to a grade. We were a large Catholic school and people moved into our community so as to take advantage of the education our parish delivered. I thanked God for that red tear.

But ultimately I was no different from any man. At first, I convinced myself that celibacy was a purification, not mere abstinence from the flesh, but a willing rejection of the world's greatest temptation, leaving God, and only God, at the center of my life.

There was a woman in the parish, Claire Schmidt, who came to me. She was a handsome woman, on the pretty side of average, a tall, raw boned Nebraskan with red hair, five years my younger. She was distraught. Her husband, John Schmidt, a businessman in nearby Kearney, had begun seeing another woman. At first he had accomplished it quietly, but when confronted by her, confirmed the tryst. The paramour, a young schoolteacher of twenty five, had convinced him to move in with her. That, he did. He left their home and joined the young woman in an apartment dedicated to their sin. He had no intention of returning home to Claire or his three children. Claire didn't know what to do. Though neither she nor her wayward husband had discussed divorce, she could only conclude that the marriage was over. This had gone on for six months. She had nowhere to turn, but to me.

I had done no significant counseling of this sort. I recommended a marriage counselor, but upon her breaking down before me in my office, I agreed to meet with her on a spiritual basis. Her husband had made it clear he was not interested, so it was simply she and I who met once a week for an hour in my office. In the fourth week of our meetings, (I had decided the counseling would not go on indefinitely) she remarked that my hands looked chapped. And indeed they were. We had experienced a rough Nebraska winter leaving the skin on my hands cracked and sore. Near the midpoint of our hour she reached into her purse and pulled from it a small tube of hand lotion from which she took, after removing the lid, a dollop of the cream and, taking my hands in hers, gently massaged in the lotion. Without warning she reached across the desk separating us, pulled me to her, then kissed me deeply.

I had experienced to that point in my life absolutely no intimacy. I set back in my chair aghast. She too, by her appearance, was stunned. A deep shade of red spread across her face and neck. She covered her mouth with her hand then gathered her purse and ran out the door.

I didn't see her the following week so awkward was the moment. Her softness, the warmth of the cream on my tired hands, the passionate kiss, seared me. I could think of nothing else.

I called her telling myself my primary mission was her wellbeing. She had come to me, had trusted me in her vulnerable state and I had taken advantage of her. She would have no part of my chivalry, stating that it was she who had initiated the moment, and did I think poorly of her for the weakness?

We agreed to meet again, the charade of counseling breaking down within minutes of her arrival. We began our own affair, consorting in her home until we took our adultery to a series of motels safely out of the way, me dressing in layman's clothes to avoid detection.

I fell in love with Claire and she with me. I was clumsy at making love. There were fourteen-year-old boys more experienced than me. But I so loved Claire that I questioned my future as a priest. I knew this must stop or I must abandon the priesthood. As suddenly as it had begun, it ended. I received a brief note from her penned in blue ink calling it off. Her husband had returned home.

I told myself it was a blessing that she left. I could now resume my priestly duties. I confessed my sin of adultery to my own confessor, and then went back to running the parish. Claire and her husband would show up on Sundays. From the pulpit I would see them together, apparently happy, and I would silently grieve.

I grew jealous of her husband asking myself why she would allow such a man back in her life. I couldn't let her go. I began following her. I knew where she worked, where she shopped. I stationed myself in parking lots across from those places obsessively thinking of us. But there was no *us*.

I received a call from her one night. She implored me to stop following her. She and her husband had reconciled. They were happy again. He was repentant and vowed to be the man and father she wanted.

I promised to leave her alone but I could not. I tried. But the stalking continued. I received an unexpected visit from the bishop who sat me down and told me in no uncertain terms I was to leave Claire Schmidt alone. She had called him and asked him to intervene. I promised him, as I did her, my behavior would change, but, once again, it did not. Ultimately, I lost my parish. I was sent to a small Hispanic church in Houston, Texas. No longer was I a pastor. I was relegated to the priestly equivalent of a flunky. I said masses, heard confessions, but I held no power. The young Hispanic pastor knew the reason for my exile. He was at all times courteous, but beyond mass and confession, I answered phones and bought groceries. I accepted my lot. I deserved it. That miraculous red tear had lost its potency.

Once a week, the young pastor allowed me Wednesday afternoon to myself. I used my time to explore Houston. I never wandered far from the church. On occasions I took a bus ride but typically I walked. During those walks I had begun wearing layman's clothes again. They were cooler and frankly I questioned my worthiness as a clergyman. I was walking on one of those Wednesdays, Claire's touch yet on my mind. Were I in Nebraska I would be stalking her at that moment, I was sure.

The neighborhood through which I took my Wednesday walks was poor and seedy, smattered with shabby liquor stores, run down tenements and houses of pornography. Turning a corner I hesitated then crawled into the smut of adult cinema as a fly would a Venetian Fly Trap just before it closed on the insect. It ate me.

My obsession turned to addiction. I replaced Claire with filth. I was no more successful at ending my Wednesday sojourns then I had been at ending my stalking of Claire. I began looking forward to Wednesdays. From the pulpit and in the confessional I cooked in my own hypocrisy. Then God intervened and put an end to my lie.

I awoke on a Wednesday and prepared a breakfast of oatmeal and scrambled eggs for Father Gutierrez and me. That morning I heard confessions, dispensing Hail Marys and Our Fathers by rote. I spent the remainder of the morning manning phones in the rectory office. At noon I ate a lunch consisting of a bowl of vegetable soup and grilled cheddar cheese on wheat toast. My weight, something I had always controlled, had gone up a bit. I dressed in street clothes and then left the rectory, the prurient destination in mind. My psyche, once focused on God's work, had become a sewer, littered with the priapic penetration of sweaty nameless flesh.

I entered the theater surreptitiously. I bought my ticket then seated myself in the dark where I belonged. An hour into the film, there came a commotion from the front of the theater. Several patrons exited immediately through the fire doors near the screen. Three others and I made our way toward the lobby. There was a man lying on the green-carpeted floor of the lobby near the concession stand. The fellow who sold tickets knelt beside him. "Call an ambulance," he said. "Now!" A woman, ostensibly an employee of the theater, sped to the concession area and picked up a phone.

The man lying on the floor motioned weekly with his left hand summoning anyone to come near. The man who knelt lowered his ear to the man's mouth.

"A priest," he said.

"He wants a priest. What should we do?"

Rather than step forward I watched the man die, his soul quite possibly bound for oblivion. Mine may as well have joined his.

The next morning I left the priesthood. I was no longer holy. I had lost the battle to sin. I left a brief note addressed to Father Gutierrez in my room telling him he was a wonderful pastor and that my leaving was by choice. I walked out carrying my suitcase, its contents the few articles of clothing I owned. I left my Roman collar on the desk in my room.

I remained in Houston. I had a small sum of money. I was resourceful. I lived at the YMCA, doing day work, until I earned a commercial license that allowed me to drive a cab for three years. I continued my descent into pornography. I saw no reason to stop now.

I had begun drinking in Nebraska. Eventually it controlled me. While in a stupor I mistook a woman walking toward me for Claire. I ran toward her bellowing "Claire! Claire!" The woman alerted an available policeman who bounced me down the street. Ultimately, I crashed my cab into a telephone pole, injuring both my fare and I.

I became homeless. I viewed life itself as my penance. I roamed Interstate 45 south of Houston, living under bridges, begging on corners, eating from dumpsters. More than once I stood atop an overpass, looking below at the speeding cars, tempted to throw myself off and end it. I told myself that if I could trade my soul for the soul of the man I let die on the cinema floor without benefit of a priest I would gladly do so. But

I was a coward, convincing myself that eternity recognized no such bargain.

During one of my several suicidal meditations at an overpass, a convertible of young people, presumably teens, sped beneath me, one of its several inhabitants shouting up at me, "Don't do it. You're still a young man." I recognized it as irreverent youth (little did he know I was actually contemplating suicide), but it was at that instant that I remembered that red tear again. I had buried it for uncountable years. It was as though a part of my being had reopened and let light in.

I became somewhat of a religious figure for the homeless up and down Interstate 45. I was homeless as well so I understood them. At times I would lead small groups in prayer. I heard no formal confessions. I never once revealed that I had been a priest. But I had always been a good listener. I could detect torment rather well. I might suggest to those wanting relief from their demons to do at least one kind act a day, or, silly as it may seem, simply pay someone a compliment. The homeless are not soulless.

I took a severe beating from a pair of young men driving a pickup truck. I was under a bridge. It was late, well after midnight. They were drunk (believe me, I knew the smell.) They insisted I was a homosexual, and upon throwing me to the ground, kicked me into unconsciousness. I awoke in the emergency room of a hospital in Galveston, Texas. Apparently someone saw me under the bridge and called for help. I stayed there 24 hours drinking coffee, seated away from people so as not to offend them with my smell. My ribs were bruised. I lost a tooth. My face was swollen and cut, but none of it was life threatening.

So there I was on Galveston Island. All those years in and around Houston and I had never seen the Gulf of Mexico. I was directed to a homeless shelter where I was given a bed for two nights, a shower and a fresh set of used, but clean wearable clothes. The shoes, black and not a color match for the brown belt I now wore, were broken in and quite comfortable. I wasted no time looking in the local paper for work. I resolved to start completely over. I was doing neither life nor myself any good the way I was. Claire, pornography and drink, God willing, were out of my life.

I had no references, no friends, but the best credential a man could ask for, that being nothing to lose, when I applied for a janitorial position at the Georgellen Club. I convinced its owner, Tom York, that I brought to the table nothing but sincerity and a willingness to work around the clock. I told him I had been a Catholic priest but had fallen through my own fault into despair.

There was a chapter of Alcoholics Anonymous on the Island (the shelter had encouraged me to investigate it) and whether he hired me or not I would be at the meeting that night. He mentioned he had been a Catholic and joked (I think it was a joke) that his soul would benefit from a priest on staff. He hired me at minimum wage on a trial basis.

That was seven years ago. I'm fifty years old now. My life is simple. I keep it that way. I attend AA meetings weekly. I live in a small but clean apartment in an alley walking distance from work. I go to mass on Sundays and sometimes pine for the life I had as a pastor. Nowadays, however, what peace of mind I have comes from helping the poor through a ministry sponsored by the shelter that helped me get started on the Island. I don't see myself ever leaving this place.

I work at the Georgellen Club. I mop floors, clean rest rooms and sweep the parking lot. The club allows me one free meal a day in addition to my wage. Neither Tom York nor I have ever brought up my past, and assuming he has told no one about me, none on the Island (save Tom) know me as anything but the hard working janitor at the Georgellen Club.

The Snake Handler

A rattlesnake bit me. It was August. I was fourteen. Two of my pals and I were exploring a wooded area near our neighborhood. I was the last one up a hill, when, to my right a bit off the beaten path, was a coiled diamond back, its triangular head drawn back, its rattles visible, making a sound like bees vibrating in a glass jar. My ankle was bare. The fangs, a pair of red hot needles, caught me just above the lip of my tennis shoe. I screamed as the snake disappeared into the underbrush.

I survived. One of my friends, Tommy York, had me sit while he tied his belt around the calf of my leg. He pulled a pocketknife from his jeans, opened it, and then cut a cross between the two red punctures. As I bled, the other boy, Phillip Lugo, ran for help.

That night in the hospital, the Holy Spirit visited me. The next day I told my parents about the experience. They assured me it was a dream, the result of a feverish delirium. But I was not mistaken. The peace that settled over me could only have come from a greater power. I went home that afternoon, my foot and leg grotesquely swollen, feeling elation beyond description.

And so changed my life. School became inconsequential. I felt no real need for learning the mundane. I became at best a marginal student, focusing instead on the contemplative aspect of life. And try as I might to dismiss that day with the rattler, I could not get out of my mind the union of snake and me, its venom coursing warmly and thoroughly throughout my being, as though it were saying "Come share with me. This will hurt for just a moment, and then you will experience truth for blessed are the bitten, it is they who know God."

I became obsessed with the venomous serpent. I studied it religiously, worrying my parents, as I suppose it should have. I graduated high school, not at all concerned with college. My mother in particular was beside herself at my decision.

I took a job with the local utility company supplying power to residential homes. My work was that of a lineman servicing overhead line. It was dangerous, but a living nevertheless. At no time did I lose my fascination for the serpent that had anointed me. Then something happened that confirmed for me what I had believed since that night in the hospital.

It was a rainy afternoon with thunderstorms preceding a spring cool front. Lightning strikes abounded, leaving a good portion of Houston without power. That day while on a pole, (another lineman and I erroneously thinking the relevant portion of cable upon which we worked had been shut off), a bolt of lightning sent a charge through the line throwing the both of us off the pole to the ground some forty feet below. Whereas I was barely bruised from the fall, the other poor fellow died on the scene, cooked from the voltage to the point that one of his limbs, the left arm, actually glowed.

The next evening I dreamt again about the serpent. Oh the wonder! The communion! My obsession grew stronger. A fellow utility worker, who hailed from Sweetwater Texas, casually mentioned to me that, as a boy, he and his uncles made a yearly pilgrimage in March to that area where they participated in what was promoted as the world's largest rattlesnake round up. How could I pass that up? I began going regularly. At first it was clumsy. I had neither the clothing nor the knowhow to participate in such an event.

I met Dorothy Goodmartin on one of my trips and we became friends. We bonded over poisonous snakes if one can believe that. Dorothy was a Pentecostal from east Texas near the Louisiana border. She was a widow, in her late forties, a good ten years older than me. Her husband, a former Pentecostal minister, had in fact died from the bite of a rattler that struck him on the neck during worship. According to Dorothy, the man died happily, united with the Lord.

Dorothy loved the snake hunts. Standing near a long deep open pit, thousands of slithering musky rattle snakes pulsing as one, I could not help but notice in Dorothy, and feel in myself, an unmistakable attraction between us. We began seeing each other. We visited each other on alternate weekends, me to her in Sink, Texas, and her to me in Houston.

That lasted several years. We parted amicably. I tried the Pentecostals for a while, mostly at the urging of Dorothy. And whereas I found that the Pentecostals handled the snakes as a measure of faith, I actually derived a pleasure, a true connection with the mystical from the venom itself. I wanted to be bitten. I enjoyed the venom. It was my drug. Life without a venom rush was, for me, simply not worth living.

By now I lived in my former home, left to me by my mother in death, my father having predeceased her. It was a small bungalow in southwest Houston, only blocks from that wooded area, now lost to development, wherein I had my encounter with the snake. Were it there now, it would be my Mecca!

In my garage, I placed a terrarium, four-foot by three-foot by three-foot, to accommodate my own rattler. I journeyed that spring back to Sweetwater where I captured and transported back to Houston in a burlap bag Otto (as I named him), a mature male western diamond back rattler, all of three feet long. I poured him into the terrarium, its bottom covered with sand, a smooth round rock in one corner and a small jar lid of water in the other. At first Otto thrashed wildly, and then coiling himself struck directly at me, leaving a trail of thick viscous venom sliding down his glass enclosure. Ultimately, he settled down, no doubt calmed by the diet of live rats and mice I fed him regularly.

I wanted for no one. My work with the utility company gave me all the human contact I needed. I much preferred sitting in a lawn chair pulled next to Otto in his terrarium, me reading a good book under the overhead light of the garage, Otto's rattles happily chirping away as a fresh rodent hid best it could in the confines of the glass prison.

And then it happened. I was bitten. While reaching for Otto's water dish, he struck me on the upper side of my right hand. Five years had gone by since I brought Otto home. I had watched him grow longer and thicker. Perhaps it was his way of letting me know he was unhappy, merely sending a message, for I am certain Otto's bite was not nearly what it could have been had he so decided.

I became ill, sick for several days, my right hand and arm swollen to a hideous purple, obscenely large and misshapen. I bore no ill toward Otto for, in truth, there was a good part of me that wanted to be bitten again, had actually designed being bitten again for I knew the risk involved in what I had done. And, as when I was a boy, some forty years before, I had never felt closer to God.

As you might imagine, I allowed Otto to bite me regularly, his large fangs penetrating my right forearm, more of a kiss than a bite. We loved each other. I fully believe that Otto came to appreciate the role he played in my life. He was my access to the heavenly. He was my portal. He was my priest!

But things end. One winter day Otto died. Like that, he was gone. At first I thought him in a state of sluggish hibernation. I had seen him act so during the colder months. But try as I might I could not rouse him. Neither could my bare arm nor the presence of a palpitating warm-blooded mouse stir him.

He was, indeed, no longer a part of my life. I mourned. I was reclusive for days, a shut in. Ultimately, I returned to work, my evenings empty. What did I do with Otto? I ate him. He and I became one.

Then came my epiphany. It was as though Otto was speaking to me from the spiritual world within which I was certain he resided. I sold my house, electing to purchase three acres of land in the rural outskirts of Houston. There I moved a small, comfortable manufactured home to the back end of the long rectangular lot. I surrounded my new home with a fence and, having inherited somewhat of a green thumb from my mother, built a garden of roses, begonias, and other colorful plants.

At the front end of the lot, adjacent to the highway, I constructed the metallic building, forty feet long by twenty feet wide to house my reptile zoo. Behind the building I constructed a shell parking lot, ample for six or seven cars that connected to the gravel driveway leading from the highway up to my house. Otto would have been proud.

Of course I needed living quarters for my snakes. I purchased two dozen of the same terrariums I had used in my garage, lining the walls of the building neatly with the glass enclosures. Financially, things had worked out well. I had retired from the utility company with thirty years of service behind me. The sale of my home in Houston not only allowed me the outright purchase of my three acres but over and above that put a substantial nest egg into my savings. And should the reptile farm, for which I would charge admission, prove profitable, I was in grand shape. I had quite simply not envisioned my life working out this wonderfully.

I required snakes. I debated variety, considering a mix of serpents: mambas, gaboon vipers, rattlers (of course) and cobras. But in the end, sticking to what I knew best, I focused in on the western diamond back. I considered returning again to

Sweetwater but by now I was an experienced snake hunter so, come the spring, in my rural area, it was rather easy to find their dens, smoke them out, and bag them. I had a few dozen within weeks. I was discriminating about the age and size of the snake I captured. Some, the rather large ones, five to six feet long, I generally passed on. They would probably outgrow their cages if they were not already over sized. Most of what I captured were in the two to four foot variety. I did build a special terrarium, one that was twelve feet long for the one super sized rattler I did catch. I simply couldn't pass that boy up. It measured six and one half feet long. Such a snake would easily impress my patrons.

I had a pretty harrowing experience while I was on one of my hunts. I was alone, as is normally the case. I came upon an opening at the top of a small bald rise. I thought surely it held a large den. And, it did. I lighted an oily rag and placed it just inside the den opening, standing off to the right, waiting for the exodus of agitated snakes. Eventually a few of the snakes did exit the opening. However, what I didn't realize is that the small hill upon which I stood was actually peppered with openings, all sharing the same mega den. In no time, rattlers surrounded me. Dozens slithered out of a myriad of holes. I immediately terminated my hunt, tiptoeing slowly and carefully away from the writhing mass, my snake boots literally dripping with venom. That was a lesson not to be forgotten.

I lived that way for ten years. Occasionally I allowed myself to be bitten. However, without Otto, who seemed to know just the right amount of venom that suited me, I came to realize that my body had not built a tolerance for the large doses of poison an inexperienced rattler could inject. Indeed, after a rather close brush with death and a skin graft on my left hand as well as an extended rehabilitation of that appendage, I decided that it was time to stop with the biting.

My rattler farm was a mild success. I never got rich from it, but there was so little overhead I actually made a profit some years or broke even in the others. Patrons did not abound. I was somewhat off the beaten path. Clientele consisted mostly of high school and college students, some of them drunk. Most times I didn't open the farm until I had an actual customer who rang a bell electronically wired to the manufactured home. Upon hearing the bell, I would walk to the reptile building and give the tour. I especially enjoyed walking people inside, shutting the door behind them, leaving all of us in almost total darkness. Once the snakes, now nearing seventy or eighty in number, sensed the presence of people in the room, they began to rattle in what I would describe as a loud, frightening hum leaving the visitors white as a sheet when I turned on the overhead lights.

Ultimately, I gave up on the reptile farm. I grew weary of it. I was approaching sixty-four years old and my fascination and passion for the reptiles was gone. I decided to turn my rattlers free. I had thought about selling them off to a local cannery that packaged and sold the exotic meat as a delicacy. But I reconsidered and bagged the eighty or so inhabitants of my reptile zoo and let them loose on the banks of a small creek that ran through my land. Watching them slither off gave me a sense of closure.

Nevertheless, I was lonely and one day out of the blue, I dialed up Dorothy Goodmartin's phone number. We chatted amicably for a few minutes, even suggesting a get together, but months went by and we never reconnected.

I took a drive to Galveston Texas for some seafood. I had never been to the Georgellen Club but had heard it was good. So there I sat with a splendid view of the Gulf, eating away at a plate of red snapper, hush puppies, and cold slaw when I saw Tommy York. Easily fifty years had gone by since that day he had performed first aid on my snake bitten leg. He was rather large and bald, not at all the thin fellow I knew, but the eyes were unmistakable. As he went by my table I said "Tommy York" not certain, but reasonably confidant that the fellow walking by was him. And it was.

"I'll be damned" he said, and then sat down with me while I ate, the both of us recounting that summer day long ago.

The Sibling

I had a bomb dropped on me at my father's funeral. He died a week before I graduated high school. He keeled over in the parking lot of a mall, the victim of a massive heart attack. My mother had died two years earlier after a lengthy bout with breast cancer. My uncle Rip, who never took a shine to me, walked me off to the side where he revealed to me that the people who raised me, Doug and Diane Anderson, were not my true parents. I was adopted. He shrugged his shoulders and said, "Sorry, kid, but it is what it is." It was 1966. I was eighteen. It was me against the world.

I went through graduation, spending a couple of weeks alone in our house. My father, who sold suits, living from month to month, had neither life nor health insurance. Any savings we had were gone, expended on my mother's medical bills.

Uncle Rip stopped by. Our discussion was frank. There was yet a mortgage on our house, a ranch style bungalow in southwest Houston. There wasn't much equity to be had, and since neither of my parents had a will, Rip suggested sale of the house and payment of the mortgage and my parents' medical and funeral bills. I was agreeable. I didn't care. And at the time, though confused by what he threw me at the funeral, I was in no hurry to find my biological parents.

"Do what you need to do," I said, " and keep anything beyond that."

The next week I signed a power of attorney, drafted by a nearby law firm, naming Rip as my agent and attorney in fact. I slept on it, packed a duffel bag, and hit the road knowing that I couldn't go far. I had one hundred dollars in my pocket.

I deliberated. I took a bus as far west as a forty-dollar fare would get me. I landed in El Paso. It seemed as good a place as any. I got a room for six dollars a night in a motel overlooking a courtyard with a pool and a scattering of lawn furniture. The Mexican man behind the desk was old. He was missing most of his front teeth. He smiled a lot. My room was small but it had a black and white TV, a window air conditioner and a shower. There was a convenience store around the corner that I visited twice a day for Vienna sausages. I drank water out of the bathroom tap. A steady stream of young women with flabby older men went in and out of two rooms across the swimming pool from me. I figured them for hookers and their "johns."

I needed a job soon and I knew it. I bought a newspaper. I hit the want ads hard. I had no job skills. I got hired to wash dishes in a Mexican restaurant for minimum wage, which at the time was about a buck fifty an hour. When I think about that job I see steam, grease, and a fluorescent light bulb. I worked my way into bussing tables. That I liked. It put me out amongst people and fresh air. After eighteen months I took on a job as a cook trainee. I learned a few things. I was generally happy. I kept my room at the motel. It was cheap. I wasn't threatened by the other tenants. We left each other alone. At times, they were actually neighborly, one of the hookers buying me a Seven Up at the soft drink machine.

I met Carmen, a waitress at work. She was brown and pouty. We had fun for a while. I was barely twenty and she was thirty. She knew how to handle men. My intentions with her were always forthright. But she had two children, a boy and a girl, by a former boyfriend. Eventually she made clear she wanted marriage. In fact, she wanted more children. I didn't want that. She accused me of taking advantage of her. That was untrue. The break up was ugly. I'd been in El Paso three years and was ready to move on. This time I had a car, a yellow 1960 Chevy Malibu with power steering and air. I headed for Phoenix for no particular reason other than it jumped out at me on the map.

I found a job as a cook in an Italian restaurant. I was beginning to tire of culinary work. I came home at night to my apartment smelling like smoke. But it paid the bills and, at the time, it is what I did. I considered finding a girlfriend. There were plenty around however I wanted no more Carmens in my life. As a distraction, I joined a gym. I'd hit my growth spurt. I was six feet, three inches tall. I was religious at the gym and, if I do say so myself, was somewhat of a physical specimen. I met a fellow there, working out, who complimented my size. He owned a bar. He asked, "I'm looking for security. Would you be interested?" I said "Hell, yes."

By security he really meant "bouncer." But that was okay by me. I couldn't have been more burned out with cooking. At this new job I was salaried. It paid twice what I made as a cook. And I had Sundays off. My other jobs, I never knew when my day off came.

I bounced for ten years. At first, I thought it was simply a matter of throwing drunks out of a bar. It was more than that. Excessive force was an issue. We had to know when to hold back even if the party thrown out was belligerent.

I met Millard and Enrique, a pair of bouncers who I teamed with at the cowboy honkytonk where I worked. Whereas Millard was more brawn than brain, Enrique was pretty sharp. However, neither man had finished high school. Both had part time work as stuntmen and that impressed me. As I approached thirty-two, I became concerned about how I would spend the rest of my life. A light was beginning to go on for me. I read a lot, and though I had a PHD in street smarts, I wanted more.

I got the message one night when a fight broke out in the bar. (I have intentionally kept out the name of the bar. Its owner, the fellow I met in the gym, was a decent man who was good to me and doesn't need his name besmirched.) In any case, a group of cowboys, drunk and trying to impress women patrons, got into it. Our job was to control the situation, but in the melee, knives came out. I took a gash across my right forearm and the palm of my left hand that sent me to the ER. Millard got his throat cut and Enrique took a wound in the stomach that grazed his liver. We all lived through it, but it was touch and go for Millard and Enrique. I got stitched up, and went to see them. Millard squeezed my hand and murmured, "get out of this trade." And Enrique did much the same. I stood by his bed where he said,

"Compadre, I have no choice. I can barely read. But you're smart. You say things over my head. Leave this business. Your future is with your mind. Adios amigo."

So, I left. I went to a local community college. It seemed crazy, but it was also time for a life decision. I was concerned about how I would make ends meet, but lo and behold, I hired on as the manager of a small pub in the student activities center. I managed it, bartended, and served as the sole security. It fit my school schedule ideally. It was open three nights a week, Thursday through Saturday, from 5:00 p.m. until 11:00 p.m. I had no real experience as a bartender, but it wasn't tough pouring beer which was the only alcohol sold there. Compared to the culture I faced in my previous job, keeping students in line was a piece of cake.

I discovered that I enjoyed the written word. I liked reading (mostly literature) and I liked writing (I kept a daily journal and dabbled with short stories about my experiences as a bouncer.) I decided I would like to teach. There were a few teachers in high school who I considered top notch and admired for the way they presented the material. I was drawn to that. I figured there were plenty of young Billy Andersons out there who needed direction.

I loved community college. I didn't realize what I had missed by not going to college but it was just as well I delayed because I wouldn't have appreciated learning had I gone right out of high school. And though Viet Nam was raging at the time I graduated high school, it wasn't a consideration for me. I had a high lottery number and my outlook on life was so indifferent that neither did college appeal to me, nor did the military frighten me into college simply to avoid the draft.

I finished community college. If I wanted to teach, I needed a four-year degree. Other than enriching my life, community college alone didn't get me where I wanted to be. For the first time in my life I felt committed to something. It felt good. It gave me purpose. I realized life as a process of smaller executed steps, goals within themselves, leading to a greater objective. I was actually feeling excited about something.

I applied to colleges just about everywhere. To my surprise, several accepted me. I'd always wanted to see the west coast. It fascinated me, so when I was accepted to a school out there, I jumped at it. I moved to Los Angeles. It was expensive at first. I wasn't a resident. But once I got past that, it was affordable. Ultimately, however, as it was in Arizona, money was a factor. During my next two and one half years, I held a series of odd jobs, coupled with a grant in aid that got me through. The day I graduated, I looked myself in the mirror and pronounced myself happy. I was thirty-six years old with a degree in Education and a minor degree in English.

I took a job teaching English to high school seniors. I devoured my work. I had a passion for life I had not experienced before. The fellow who washed dishes, who broke noses as a bouncer, seemed, at times, like some character I'd read about, but who wasn't me.

I taught twenty-eight years. I never married. I had three girlfriends (not counting Carmen) all of them wonderful, all of them willing to try to understand me. But I had lived so long by myself that the confines of another person sharing all my time was impossible for me to incorporate. They wanted permanency. I did not. That part of me hadn't changed. Each of the breakups was painful.

I retired. I lived alone. I was solitary. I had time to think. I ruminated on my past. I cogitated on what Uncle Rip told me. Somewhere out there was my gene pool. Somewhere out there was true family. Somewhere out there was my blood.

I flew to Houston. I got a room. I looked up Laura. She was my alternate universe cousin. She was Uncle Rip's daughter. I called her. She invited me over. We hadn't seen each other in forty-eight years. She had changed. She was no longer gorgeous. She was no longer cheerleader trim. She was wrinkled. She was heavy. She puffed cigarettes. She was Uncle Rip in female form. We visited. She told me Uncle Rip was dead. She had no idea who my biological parents were. She asked me "Does it matter so much? Aren't we still family?" I told her we were family. I told her I would stay in touch. We hugged. I felt myself lie. I felt Laura lie. I doubted we would see each other again.

I flew back to Los Angeles. I began a novel. I wrote. I thought. I was obsessed with who I was. My writing suffered. I knew what the problem was. I got back on a plane. I flew back to Houston. I rented an apartment short term. I needed closure. I hired an attorney. She was middle aged. She spelled it out to me. She could track my biological family down if and only if they wanted to be found.

So I holed up in my apartment waiting for things to happen. I had heard stories of people such as myself who had found true family only to be disappointed. My adoptive parents had certainly been good to me. They did the best they could with what they had. I never once felt unloved by them. How many people can say that?

I rented a car. I drove my old neighborhood. I toured my old schools. I reminisced. I viewed my past in a positive light.

I got a call. It was my attorney. She set a meeting with a judge. I expected good news. I showed up on time. I had on my best face. The judge took us in her office. She closed the door.

"Mr. Anderson," said the judge, "you are familiar with how this process of locating biological family works?"

I looked at my attorney who sat next to me, both of us across the desk from a female judge.

"Somewhat," I confirmed.

"Well, your attorney has run the Texas Registry Service and found no match. You don't know the name of your parents or any siblings?"

"I do not."

"Do you know the name of the agency through which you were adopted?"

"I do not, and Ms. Jackson here and I have been over that."

The judge pointed to a file resting on her desk.

"Ms. Jackson has petitioned this court on your behalf. That's your file. It's all in there. Ms. Jackson, can you show me good cause for opening this file and letting Mr. Anderson have a look inside?"

My attorney looked at me.

"Nothing immediate or dire," I said. "My adoptive parents and uncle are gone. I have a cousin through that family, but honestly, there's nothing between her and me, and she knows nothing of my biological family. I have no one. Put yourself in my shoes."

I debated grabbing the file and running out of the room. Instead, the judge did as much for me as my face sank.

"I'm stepping out for a moment to deal with another matter," she said. "This file is not to be opened." She got up from her desk. I sensed sympathy. She shut the door. My attorney turned away from me. She feigned distraction. I opened the file. I read the name "York." I heard the judge cough as she opened the door. She went back to her desk. My attorney and I left the courthouse. I thanked her for her work. I wrote her a check. She and the judge were decent people.

I took the name. I wrote it down. I checked the directory. There was no one by that name. I figured them for Houston. I called my attorney. She confirmed they were local. She stopped it there. I hired a private investigator. His name was Buddy Locke. He charged one hundred dollars an hour plus expenses. He promised to find my family. He convinced me he was good.

I waited three weeks. He called me daily. He briefed me on his findings. He was coming up short. How far did I want him to go? I debated renewing my lease. Frustration was clouding my mind. I missed my condo in LA. I had one week to decide. I got a phone call. It was Buddy Locke.

"I don't have your guy," he said, "but I have a guy who might have your guy."

So I called August Spivey, a colleague of Locke, a fellow private "I". He knew someone named "York". The man owned the Georgellen Club. It was in Galveston Texas. I asked did I owe him? He said it was free. He owed Buddy Locke a favor.

I drove to Galveston where I found the Georgellen Club. I went in cold. This fellow, Tom York, had no idea I was coming. Here I was, a man he didn't know from Adam, who was going to tell him we were brothers. I considered calling the whole thing off. Even if these people were family we had no bond, no common experience. It was noon. I took a table. I ordered a salmon salad. I looked around for somebody who resembled me. The waiter, a young man, brought me my check.

"Is Mr. York here today?" I asked.

"Sure," he said. "Was the service ok?"

I assured him it was. I tipped him well. He went for Tom York. A minute later he and a large bald man appeared near the bar. The waiter pointed at me. Tom York strolled over. It was like looking into a mirror. He was large, over six feet, muscular, and about my age.

"I'm York," he said, " how can I help you?"

"Can you give me ten minutes? I have an interesting story to tell you."

So Tom York sat down. I told him who I was.

"I'm not here for anything monetary. I'm a retired teacher. I've got a good life going. But not knowing who I am has been eating at me for a long time."

When it was over, York sat back in his chair. I could tell he was all business, but my revelation shook him.

"How did you find me?" he asked.

I told him how I ran up against a wall, and how I pulled the name "York" from my adoption record. I told the story in a way that put the judge and my lawyer out in the hall when I dug in the file. Other than that, I came clean with him.

"So, you dropped in to see if we are really your family?" he asked.

"Yes," I said. "Wouldn't you want some closure if you found out you had another family?"

He motioned me into his office where our conversation went on another two hours. We studied each other.

"And you were a bouncer?" he asked.

"Among other things," I said

"Well, we have the bar business in common," he said and laughed.

I could tell he didn't know what to make of it. Our shared father was dead and our mother lived in a retirement village up Interstate 45 a bit.

"If this is uncomfortable, or if you think this will upset your mother….our mother, I'll go back to LA. Say so and I'm gone."

"I'll do this," he said. "I'll contact mother. If she denies this, it's all over. And if she acknowledges you as her son, but doesn't want to meet, it's all over then as well."

We agreed. He took my phone number at the rental apartment. He would call me in forty-eight hours or less. If I hadn't heard from him by then, this meeting never took place, I would never come back into the Georgellen Club, and I would not go near the woman I thought to be our mother.

"That's only fair," I said and shook his hand.

I drove back to Houston. Part of me wanted to meet my biological parent, part of me didn't. What if she rejected me again? It was odd sitting across from Tom York, someone I was certain, just by his looks, was my brother. And yet, we were complete strangers. It was easily the most unnatural I've ever felt.

The call came in the following afternoon. He confirmed that his mother had indeed given birth to a son she and her husband later put up for adoption. I was to meet Tom York at the retirement center the next morning. We were on. Something was going to happen.

I didn't sleep a wink that night. I tried, but my mind was jumping from one scenario to the next. I arose at 5:00 a.m. and showered. I was tired but the cold water refreshed me. I ate a slice of cantaloupe and drank a cup of black coffee. I debated not showing up. I was beset with anxiety. But I'd come too far for that.

I got out in rush hour traffic in my rental car, a Ford Escape. Houston traffic was bad when I grew up here and it had only gotten worse in the forty-eight years I'd been gone. But heavy traffic, the kind you encounter in Houston and LA, made me a seasoned urban driver.

I arrived at the retirement center at 7:30, the time Tom York had instructed. I pulled into a nice, upscale campus of buildings, gardens and swimming pools. People were walking, jogging, riding bicycles and carrying golf clubs. It was far more attractive than I had expected. I pulled into a parking space and immediately saw Tom York at the front door. I waived at him as I stepped out of my car. At the door of the center we shook hands.

"Are you sure you and your mother want to do this?" I asked.

"I am," he said, "and so is she," he stated.

"Do you mind if I ask how she reacted?" I said.

"I caught her off guard, but it went well. Let's go," said York.

We entered into a first rate building, and then signed in with a young attractive woman at the front desk.

"They're eating," said York. "This way."

We walked down the corridor, took a right turn and stopped at the entrance to a posh dining area.

"Let me see if I can pick her out," I said, me believing blood to be thicker than water. I wanted to divine my way to my mother.

"Go ahead," he said. "I'll wait here."

I went into the dining room. These were healthy, retired seniors, tanned and energetic. They ate and visited cheerfully. I looked around. I felt something, an intuition perhaps, pull me to the right. A tall, thin, woman with short silver hair, wearing casual slacks and a long sleeved white blouse stood and waived. I walked forward slowly. I saw her eyes focus, I suspect thinking I was her son, Tom. As I got closer I heard, " That's her, you got it right." It was Tom York who had slipped up beside me. The woman's eyes melted as did her posture. She bent at the waist, folding her arms as though she were cold. She motioned us over.

"Mother," said Tom York, "I would like to present Bill Anderson. I believe he is your son and my brother."

Time stopped. I thought I would faint. The night I got cut as a bouncer, losing enough blood to require a transfusion, I never came close to passing out. The three of us sat down in unison at the table. The event had proven overwhelming for all of us.

"I don't know where to start," she said.

"My name," I said, "what's my name?"

"We were going to name you Lee," she said. "Lee York."

I watched as her lower lip quivered, and then she broke down.

"I'm so sorry," she said. "We were young, in high school, unmarried. I got pregnant. Our parents pushed us toward adoption. We married after we graduated high school. We were so young. Please don't hate me. Please."

Tom York placed his hand on her shoulder. I was tempted to do the same but didn't think it appropriate. We waited, each of us silently collecting ourselves.

"So tell me about your life," she requested. "You have no idea, how much your father and I thought about you, talked about you, regretted giving you up."

I launched into my story, telling her and Tom I had grown up right here in Houston. My adoptive parents, I assured her, were good people who I loved and who loved me. I was short-changed nothing. My life had been somewhat of an Odyssey, culminating in a profession as a teacher.

"I'm happy," she said, then filled me in on her husband, now deceased, and Tom, who they had in the year after they were married.

We spent an exhausting, wonderful morning together, the three of us pausing for intermittent spells of crying. Tom York was hard as flint, I read that the moment we met two days before, but even he had a trickle of moisture on his cheeks.

I decided it was time to wrap it up. Peace settled over me almost immediately. I was whole.

"Please don't let this be the end of things," she asked plaintively as she took my large right hand into both of hers. "You are my son. You and Tommy are my sons."

I promised her and Tom we would always be family; that I would never lose touch with them; that everything would be all right. I hugged her warmly. I felt myself tell the truth. I felt my mother tell me the truth.

The Runner

I'll cut to the chase. I killed for a living. And you wouldn't know it if you'd seen me when I was young.

I was a fat kid on my way to becoming an obese adult. I loved to eat. Actually, I loved to gorge. My mother, raised on a farm, was accustomed to cooking large meals for her father and brothers who worked long physical hours in their fields. I ate like a farmer but I, being a sedentary urban kid, packed on the pounds.

My parents were on opposite ends of the cosmic spectrum. My mother, a practicing Catholic, believed (or so she professed) in a creator God involved intimately in the lives of each and every one us. My father, a robust atheist, believed in nothing beyond this life. He referred to Jesus Christ as "J" Christ. However he allowed, as per the traditions of my mother's religion, my two younger brothers and I to be raised as Catholics.

Needless to say, this created its own form of tension. Whereas my father did not shove his atheism down our throats, neither did he hesitate to express his disdain for religion when asked. The result was a family torn, but I must give my parents credit, for beyond that fundamental difference, they got along well. Ultimately, to satisfy what I think was a bargain between my parents, upon our graduation from Catholic high school, our mother made clear to us that we no longer owed her the pretense of belief in the Almighty if indeed we held no such belief. This presented no great difficulty for me. I, like my father, simply did not believe in God. (There was one moment of weakness, me in high school, when my father stated to me that he actually wished he could believe in a God but, based on what he had seen in life, did not possess the faculty to do so.) My brothers, however, did suffer psychological problems resulting in drug and alcohol dependency. I liken such mental unrest to the storms that come in the spring of the year marking the transition from winter to summer. Until you fall fully one way or the other, either as a believer or not, the mind will never rest. And so it was that I graduated high school, settled in my atheism, and severely overweight.

The military cured my weight problem. It was 1968, Viet Nam was in full swing, and I, above the objection of my parents, and not waiting for a call from my draft board, enlisted in the marines. (My mother got it in her mind there was a girl I was trying to impress but that was not the case. I was simply bored, not wanting to go to college, and naïve, despite my father's admonition of the altering effect of war.) I lost weight fast, near one hundred pounds, to the point that my two brothers didn't recognize me upon my return to Houston after the war.

But it was in Viet Nam that I learned how to kill, both efficiently and comfortably. Because I neither believed in God nor a moral order in the universe, I saw life as a competition of forces, neither good nor evil, but composed of relative strengths and weaknesses. Taking a life wasn't a moral question, but one of physics, wherein a knife thrust into a man tore at flesh and bone and admittedly terminated a life but had no effect beyond that. There was simply and mathematically, at that point of death, one less human on the planet. I returned from Viet Nam without one scintilla of guilt about my service.

However, the adjustment to civilian life was more difficult than I anticipated. One day I was in a jungle, barbarism the norm, then forty-eight hours later I was home in Houston thinking about college on the GI Bill in the fall.

I was a good student. The military instilled within me a sense of discipline. However, I was estranged from the students around me as I was a twenty-one year old freshman at the local university surrounded by, but for a sprinkling of other vets, eighteen year olds with whom I had nothing in common. I had enough foresight to choose accounting for practical purposes and psychology as I wanted to know what made me and the people around me tick. My grades were good, much better than what they would have been had I entered college right out of high school.

But there was an incipient tension that wouldn't go away. And it became worse. I was beginning to feel what I suspected was the same struggle within my troubled brothers. Was there a God? And what did such a being expect? I went to therapy offered by the school and support group meetings involving campus vets who were going through, I assume, post traumatic stress disorder. My problem wasn't a sense of horror from what I had engaged in while in Viet Nam. My problem was that I found myself missing those bloody nights, which was compounded by a subtle yet relentless conscience I had buried long ago. The therapy helped little. By chance I discovered running.

My schedule was demanding. I was in school Monday through Friday, and, even though I was going to school on the government's dime, I found it necessary to work nights and weekends. The combination of work and school exhausted me, but I was young and in relatively good shape. I had two jobs, one of them full time as a health club attendant in a local YMCA, the other as night watchman on the weekends at a shopping mall. The job at the YMCA required that I work nights from 4:00 p.m. until midnight. I slept little. I normally arrived back at my apartment by 12:30 and went straight to bed, resulting in at best 5-6 hours of sleep.

One night, my car (I bought a used Chevy out of the newspaper) in the shop for repair, I decided that in lieu of waiting in the dark for a bus I would run home. My apartment was less than two miles away and I took off as soon as I left the "Y." It was a humid night in February. I ran the entire distance, in tennis shoes and janitorial pants, and when I arrived home, soaked in sweat, I showered and slept like a rock. After that I began running home every night, electing to leave my car parked at my apartment, taking the bus to work, but running home afterwards. I braved spring rain, heat, any weather Houston could throw at me in exchange for the sense of calm that my night run gave me.

The following summer, my schedule the same, I fit running into my regimen. It worked to calm me but I had become, in my civilian days, an insomniac waking religiously at 3:00 a.m. feeling a tension that could only be relieved by the offerings of the jungle. Nevertheless, I resisted my urge to kill, and finished school with my degrees in accounting and psychology.

I went to work in corporate America (the oil industry) but found the culture a bit too restrictive. I was not prone to authority issues in the marines, but I simply found such an environment in my civilian life stifling. So, at age thirty, I started my own accounting firm, a rather small affair comprised of an associate accountant to catch the overflow, a secretary (Nadia) and me. Nadia has stayed with me to this day.

Work coupled with running served as somewhat of a distraction to allay my fevered mind, but the insomnia remained. I began running long distances from 4:00 until 6:00 in the morning, gaining some relief, but never enough to satisfy the joy I felt those jungle nights in Viet Nam.

Ultimately, I snapped. I needed to kill. The marathons, the logged miles, the complex carbs were simply not enough. I did something incredibly foolish. I ran an ad in a mercenary magazine holding myself out as someone willing to do any and all odd jobs. I got a call from a man I met a week later at a fast food place on the north side. He could have been a cop or a freak (yeah, like I wasn't) but he was for real and for ten thousand dollars, which he deposited in a shed in the country, a fellow disappeared from mother earth, no questions asked.

And it was so convenient. I had my own business. I could come and go as I pleased. I simply told Nadia I was taking a few days off. I was an accountant for God's sakes. No one came close to suspecting me although in the darker circles of the Houston underworld I gained a reputation as a reliable, discreet, independent contractor. I made money, yes, but I satisfied an urge that had taken over my life many years before. I continued running, I continued my accounting business, and I continued my "dark" trade (as I came to think of it.) Somehow, it just kept going and going right along like a smooth running machine. I lived that way for years.

Then irony came along. I made a mistake. I allowed the personal to trump the professional. I did business with a friend. Tommy York came to me. He wanted someone removed. It was an old acquaintance of his, now the aging suitor of a young woman who Tommy had pledged to protect. I didn't want the job. I didn't need the job, but I was weak and should have known better. I should have said "no" but I went ahead, took the work, and completed it, making it clear to Tommy that, in this case, business trumped friendship. But that wasn't true. I'd taken the job out of friendship. If Tommy ever got cold feet, or was linked to the disappearance of the man he wanted gone, could I put a bullet in Tommy and toss him into the Gulf of Mexico? There are times when I look into the mirror and ask myself what I was thinking.

I went for a run in Galveston. I loved running the beach in the dark hours of the morning, and then watching the sun wash over the planet turning it orange. I normally departed my office in Houston on Friday afternoon, leaving Nadia to run things. I typically arrived in Galveston at around 5:00 p.m., checked into my favorite hotel on the beach, and then ran Saturday and Sunday mornings. I had never been a regular at the Georgellen Club, and now that I had done dark business with Tommy, made it a point to sever any and all connection I had with him or the club.

I took off running on Sunday morning right at 4:00 a.m. on a beautiful October day. The wind was from the north, bringing with it a dry cool scent of fall. As I ran I daydreamed, alternating most times between anxiety and nirvana. I was a bad man now. I was someone worth loathing. I was odd. I was aberrant. Or was I simply a fellow who recognized the silliness of moral dilemma? Life was what you wanted and what you could take and what you could get away with. I fluctuated often, as I ran, between the darkness and light within me.

I was near finishing the run. The sun had come up. I was ready for a shower, a healthy breakfast, and then a drive back to Houston where I would stop by my office and do a little work, a wonderful way to close the weekend.

As I ran past the Georgellen Club, on the way back to my hotel, I noticed a woman getting into a car in the parking lot of the club, not one hundred feet away. She appeared to be in her thirties, and with her were a pair of dogs, leashed and panting. My first impression was that she had taken them for a walk on the beach. I thought nothing more of it, but as I continued onward heard, first, a series of growls, and then felt hot breath on my left leg. I went down without knowing what was happening. I managed to roll onto my back just as one of the dogs (pit bulls, now that I saw them up close) sank its teeth deeply into my left calf. Its jaws locked. I felt my calf begin to tear. The other pit was at my neck, thwarted by my extended left arm. It too felt the crushing pressure of the dog's incredible strength. With my right arm I zipped open my fanny pack and pulled from it, with what little focus I had left, the revolver I carried with me at all times. I pumped a pair of slugs into the throat of the pit whose bare teeth were edging closer and closer to my face. It yelped, ran a few feet, and then fell over. I did the same to the dog at my leg, firing directly, and at close range, into its muzzle, emptying my gun as I leaned forward. It fell beside of me, into a heap, its canine smell (or the scent of my blood) invading my nostrils. I heard a woman scream, and then I passed out.

I awoke in John Sealy Hospital. The next several days were spent in delirium. I lapsed in and out of consciousness. Tom York visited me, or so I thought. Was his visit a dream? I don't know.

"You don't intend," he asked, "to get even with Julia Jax, do you?"

"I'm an assassin, Tommy. It's business with me. Remember? But what if I did intend payback?"

"I couldn't allow that, Phil. That's where I'd draw the line between you and me."

"We did business, Tommy," I said. "I made the terms clear."

Once lucid, I summoned a nurse. It was night and the hospital was quiet. I couldn't tell if Tom had been in my room or not. Had I actually spoken to him? Was someone with him in the room? What did they hear? Were Tommy and I enemies now? Could I trust him? Could he trust me? I regretted ever taking the job but what was done was done. I was an experienced professional assassin but even the best made mistakes.

"I lost my leg," I said flatly.

"How did you know that?" asked the nurse.

"I felt it go when the dog bit down," I said. "How long was I out?"

"The better part of four days," she said.

"Did anyone visit me?"

"Not that I know of. I'll check," she answered.

She returned shortly and confirmed that no one recalled anyone visiting me. The following morning I asked the day nurse who stated the same. Just before lunch my surgeon, Dr. Goode, visited me.

"The leg's gone, you know that, I hear," he said.

"I do," I answered.

"How are you going to be with that?"

"Legless," I stated wryly, "but I'll deal with it."

He nodded at my bandaged left arm.

"You managed to keep that."

"Yes," I sighed. "Are the dogs dead?"

"I have no idea."

He briefed me on the healing, the prosthetic leg, and the therapy.

A year later I began running on my artificial limb. It took me several months to get back in shape. I stayed out of Galveston, not wanting to cross paths with Tom York. I gave up the dark trade. I was sixty-four and too old for such business. The anxiety remained. I preferred to believe in nothing, but the struggle between good and evil had once again taken up residence in my psyche.

I had no idea what Tom York had up his sleeve. Would he get me before I got him? Two years after my stay in the hospital I was walking along Main Street in downtown Houston. Tom was walking toward me, his broad shoulders and bald head towering above the crowd. We made eye contact, but said nothing as we passed each other.

The Ghost

We come. We go. And some of us get caught in between. I am a ghost. I walk the Georgellen Club. This is how it happened.

My name is George Jax. Or, should I say it was George Jax? I joined the U.S. Navy fresh out of high school, two weeks after my eighteenth birthday. It was June of 1942, and America was gearing up for World War II. I couldn't wait to enlist. I was young, I loved my country, and I wanted to impress women. I fought in the Pacific. I found out early how horrible war is. I saw men die. I saw men blown to bits.

After the war, upon my discharge, rather than returning to Minnesota, I settled in Houston Texas. While in the Pacific, I grew to like hot weather. Give me heat and humidity any day over the ice and snow. I remember once, when I was a boy, my father, a high school math teacher, and I were driving by a lake near our home in Saint Paul. It was winter, and out on the frozen lake were several ice fishing shacks that the locals would sit in while they fished through a hole in the ice.

"Son," said my father, "were I to do it all over, I would have moved your mother and myself to the South: Dallas, or Houston, maybe Atlanta. I predict that someday there will be opportunity in those cities. Don't get stuck out on that lake drinking beer to keep warm while you wait for a fish to come along."

So that's what I did. I took my father's advice and decided Houston would be home. I had no skills. The GI bill was available but I never liked school (despite my father being an educator) and I was in no hurry to buy a home. The war had changed me. I saw life as precious and fleeting. I was young and didn't want to settle down. I wanted fun. I wanted life. Marriage, family and career could wait.

I rented an apartment in the bohemian part of town. My father liked that I had remained in the South. (I reminded him of our drive by that frozen lake.) He and my mother sent me three hundred dollars with the assurance that if Houston didn't work out, I always had a home to return to.

I bought a car, a used Ford Fairlane for seventy-five dollars from a car lot on the Gulf Freeway. The fellow who sold me the car was a fast-talker, but that car ran like a top. And my apartment was cheap. It had no air conditioning, but I didn't care. The world was my oyster.

Initially, I went to work as a laborer. I was in good shape and came from a strong gene pool, so picking up heavy lumber and concrete was simply part of a hard day's work. I figured it for short term until I found the occupation that I was best suited for. At that point in my life, I wanted a job that simply paid the bills.

Growing up in Minnesota, I was introduced early to a " hands on" approach to life. My father was, despite his academic calling, somewhat of a frustrated mechanic. He had a shop in the garage and by the time I was twelve he and I were working on our car or fixing our neighbors' lawn mowers. We rewired the house one summer and re-roofing our home was just another exercise in self-sufficiency. With that type of background, I was more than prepared to take on any job opportunity. The Navy also had instilled within me a wealth of confidence.

The opportunity presented itself in the form of tragedy.

We were on the job one day when a frontend loader, driven by a young Mexican boy, flipped over and crushed him. I saw it happen. He was coming down a steep incline when the brakes failed. There were a dozen or more of us at the bottom of the hill and when we saw that he was out of control, (he was waiving at us to get out of the way), we all ran for cover behind a small grove of large trees. The front-end loader rolled right, throwing him out, only to bury him beneath tons of steel and rubber.

I was shaken, but having seen death in the Pacific, was somewhat hardened to such horror. The following Monday when work resumed, no one wanted the task of working the same machine that had killed the young boy. I volunteered. I lied a bit telling the construction foreman that I had driven heavy machinery. I had not, but within thirty minutes I figured out the ignition and the workings of the loader, and by noon of that day was fast at work moving earth and debris. It meant a raise of one dollar an hour. Nowadays, I doubt that I could get away with such a stunt.

I stayed in the construction industry for several years. My car eventually wore out, so I replaced it with a Harley Davidson motorcycle. By now I was becoming quite the nonconformist. Compliments of a shop in Manila, I had acquired a tattoo of the Stars and Stripes while in the Navy (on my right shoulder.) I grew a beard (jet black.) I wore a bandana to hold back my long hair. I began touring with a motorcycle club on the weekends. I loved being a rebel. It was a part of me that I hadn't realized, but enjoyed developing, despite my entire family's disapproval. (I drove my bike to Minnesota for a visit, beard, bandana and all, to find my parents, three sisters, and grandparents put off by my new lifestyle.)

I turned twenty-five. My job as a heavy machine operator was by now making me good money. I loved Houston, especially the part of town that I lived in, full of artists and poets and small bars. I discovered somewhat of an artistic bent that pushed me in another direction. I was sitting at the table of my efficiency apartment (the same as the one I had moved into four years before.) The window was open on a hot August evening. I had no television, and was not interested in reading that night, a habit that, despite my youthful indifference to learning, resulted in my walls being lined with bookshelves full of books about philosophy, fiction, and history. I began doodling with a pencil upon the back of a grocery bag. I drew the view I had of my apartment—its kitchen, the bed, the books, all within a few steps of where I sat. Drawn upon the brown grocery sack, I must say that the rendition of my apartment was rather accurate. I framed the picture and hung it over my bed, one of the few spaces left open due to the crush of bookshelves. I deemed myself an artist, and that is how I met Ellen Carpenter.

I decided that, if I was to be an artist, formal training was a must. Having watched and respected my father's work as a teacher, I realized that raw talent, by itself, was insufficient, and that form and substance were an essential union in artistic development. I took an art class at a nearby junior college. I hadn't been in any type of school setting (unless you count gunnery school) since high school. That was seven years ago.

The first night in class I considered leaving at the break, but I disappointed myself at how easily I had almost given up and went back in. My instructor was a nice, polite, effeminate fellow named Steve Slive. He was quite patient with me and the several other people in the class. That first night, we had been asked to bring with us any piece of artwork we had done. My only "art" was the sketch I had made of my room on the grocery bag. Slive was encouraging and I believe he was also sincere when he told me I had potential. Over the next six weeks, as he trained us in technique, he pointed out my strengths and weaknesses. He emphasized that one could paint as a hobbyist or as a real artist, but the latter required both talent and dedication. There was no dabbling in art for the true artist.

On the night I finished the class, I thanked Steve Slive for his instruction and said goodbye to the few students who had stayed the entire six weeks. I hopped on my motorcycle entertaining the notion that I might have a future as an artist. I was determined to put in the work. I had already turned a corner of my apartment into a small studio with easel, light, and a canvas floor cover.

Across the street from the community college was a convenience store I had begun stopping in after class for a quick sandwich and drink as I had been coming to class on Tuesdays and Thursdays directly from work. The fellow (its owner) behind the counter was a tall white man who had come to know me visually due to my regular stop after class. I parked my motorcycle, walked in, nodded, and then went back to the cooler for my sandwich and pint of milk. Standing at the back was a woman whose attention was also on the cooler. I waited for her to finish when, in the reflection of glass, I saw a man walk into the store brandishing a gun. It all happened quickly.

"Ma'am," I said, then, upon getting her attention, "don't look up. This store is being robbed."

I stepped behind her so as to put myself between her and the action at the front of the store. She did as I told, keeping her eyes straight ahead on the cooler, but remarking softly upon seeing what I saw in its reflection "Oh my!"

Then it broke loose. The owner immediately produced a gun from beneath the counter and began firing at the robber who fired back, both exchanges coming from close range.

"Get down," I said, then pushed her to the floor, at the same time feeling a hot thud and a tear rip across my left hand. I looked at my hand. Half of it was gone. What was left was dripping red onto the floor! The smell of gunpowder filled the room. I heard the woman scream.

I woke up in the ER of Ben Taub Hospital. I had intermittent memories of a fast ride and a screaming siren. The first time I was fully aware of my surroundings was in a hospital room several days later. My left arm was wrapped, I was in a bed, and my hand (what used to be my hand) throbbed. At first I thought I was back in the navy, wounded in combat.

The hospital staff informed me that I had lost most of my left hand in the robbery. Remaining were my thumb and index finger. Having seen, first hand in war, flesh and bone torn away from its owner, I took my loss fairly well. I had several days to think about it while lying in the hospital bed. Since my hand was wrapped, I couldn't see the damage, my only recollection being the bloody mess I stared into at the convenience store. On the day I was to leave the hospital, as I sat fully dressed in a chair next to my bed, a young woman stepped in after softly tapping on the door. She identified herself as Ellen Carpenter, the woman with me the night of the robbery.

"I couldn't go on with my life," she said, "without thanking you. I tried several times to stop in, but the hospital said you weren't ready for guests." She looked at my bandaged left hand. "How bad is it?"

"It's gone," I said. "Well, most of it's gone."

"I'm so sorry," she said. "I don't know what to say. You may have saved my life."

"Don't thank me," I said. "It happened fast. There was no thought in my move. I reacted. I'm glad you didn't get hurt."

"Is there anything I can do to help you?"

"You can give me a ride home," I suggested. "I have no idea where my motorcycle is."

I was rolled in a wheelchair to the front of the hospital where Ellen had pulled around her car. I'd been in a hospital bed five days and in that short amount of time had lost a noticeable amount of strength in my legs.

At my apartment I invited Ellen inside as she had volunteered to help me track down my motorcycle. I phoned my boss, who assured me that my job was still there and that they would work with me while I healed.

Ellen then drove me to the convenience store where a different fellow gave me the number of the compound that was holding my bike. Both the clerk and the robber who had exchanged gunfire were injured and were in the hospital as well. Ellen paid to have my motorcycle released.

"Can you drive that?" she asked.

"I don't think I can," I answered. "I didn't consider what the loss of my hand would mean."

"I have an idea," she said.

With that she made a phone call from a pay phone to a fellow waiter at the restaurant where she worked. Inside of thirty minutes a muscular black man was dropped off where my bike had been released.

"If it's ok with you, Andre can drive your motorcycle home for you. You and I can follow in my car."

And so we did. I thanked Andre and tried to tip him but neither Ellen nor Andre would have anything of it. I settled into my apartment, brooding at the prospect of dealing with life on one and a half hands.

Work became an immediate problem. The construction company that employed me was quite generous, picking up my hospital bills and assigning me to the office. (I filed suit against the convenience store and received a small, negotiated sum that I gave back to my boss to offset the hospital bills he had paid for me.) But the business was small, family run, and the two ladies who ran the office were the wife and sister of the owner. There was no future in answering phones or filing time sheets, and once the bandages came off (I had seen on two other occasions with my doctor how badly I was impaired) it became clear that my days of driving heavy machinery were over. Fortunately, I could still drive my motorcycle. My left hand looked like a claw, my thumb and index finger forming a human pincer. I quit, and decided to throw all my energy into my art. Stranger things have happened. Why couldn't I succeed as an artist?

Two months after Ellen had driven me home from the hospital, I received a phone call, out of the blue, from her. I was flattered. I hadn't given her much thought. I was dwelling continuously during that period on myself. She invited me to lunch, which I accepted. We met at an Italian restaurant not far from where I lived and different from the restaurant she worked at as a waitress. I pulled up on my motorcycle and noticed her waiving from a table on the patio of Gene's, a nice little eatery I was familiar with.

To that point, I'd had two girlfriends, one in high school, and one since landing in Houston. Both were nice, and attractive by my standards, but I (and they) knew there was nothing long-term in the offing. Ellen did not have their looks, but she had a personality that radiated character and loyalty. As the meal progressed she nodded to my bike.

"I see you brought your wheels," she remarked. "I'm on foot, you know. I'd take a ride if offered."

We had a wonderful afternoon. I took her riding in the country south and west of Houston. While at lunch I mentioned that I had left my construction job and launched into the life of an artist. My chosen art form was the pastoral. I enjoyed panoramas of farmland. On the way out of town we stopped at her apartment where she grabbed a Polaroid camera. We made several stops on country roads that gave us beautiful opportunities. Ellen shot pictures. She enjoyed photography and dabbled in it as a hobby. After getting the pictures developed, she gave me a set, suggesting that I use them for my paintings.

We eventually moved in together. We compromised and rented a larger apartment near where she worked. I missed my old apartment, having grown attached to the small private world it afforded me. I had also become a creature of habit, uncomfortable with change. But Ellen and I made it work. She went off to her job at night. I painted out on a fenced patio that sat beyond our tiny kitchen. I felt pressure to produce as an artist. I didn't like the idea of being supported by someone else, especially a woman. There were times when my art suffered. Other times, it flowed naturally. I discovered that I had a rather passionate, volatile disposition that I rationalized as being the temperament of an artist.

We lived that way for six years. I sold some paintings, enough to make me feel like an artist, but not enough to make a living. We began scratching and clawing a bit at each other. We both knew that we needed different paths. Ellen, at age twenty-eight, did not want to waitress the rest of her life, and I was coming to grips with the realization that I would never be anything more than a hobby painter. I didn't know what to do. I was thirty-one and had only my naval background. I regretted not having gone to school on the GI bill, and could probably have still pursued that, but I didn't have it in me to go back to school at my age. That, coupled with my mangled hand, threw me into a depression that I sometimes took out on Ellen. Things were looking bleak for us when, Ellen hatched an idea.

"Let's take a ride," she suggested. And like many times before, when things were blowing up, we jumped on my motorcycle and rode.

We took, at Ellen's direction, I45 South, to Galveston. I knew Galveston well. She and I often biked there for an occasional day at the beach. We went west along the seawall, the waves soothing my worried mind.

"Here," she said, "right here."

She pointed to an abandoned building that had seen its day, north of the sea wall, its length facing the Gulf of Mexico. We jumped off my bike and walked the premises.

"What do you see?" she asked.

"Sand and sea," I answered.

"Come on," she urged, "show some imagination."

I shrugged.

"I see a restaurant," she said. "Look."

She walked around the front of the old building, pointing here and there where the main dining area would go.

"And over here would be a deck and in here the kitchen. Parking could be out back. We're still young, George, but things are getting stale for the both of us. We need a shot of energy. Let's do this. We have nothing to lose."

Ellen was right. Her view of life was still young and fresh and she refused to let that go. I, on the other hand, had become complacent and unimaginative. It was no wonder my art was going nowhere. I recalled the war, seeing life blown out like a flame in the wind, how precious time was.

"What the hell," I said. "But how do we pay for this?"

We had, between us, ten thousand dollars in savings, most of it thanks to Ellen. We did what any small business people would do. We made a plan, crude, but thorough, and with it obtained a loan. We moved fast on the land and found out that the estate of the deceased owner, a lawyer at one time, wanted rid of it so as to pay off other estate debts. The widow of the deceased man was the estate executrix, a pleasant woman, who dealt with us straight up fair and square. With a loan for one hundred thousand dollars, our savings, and sweat, we got it done. Our little bar restaurant was beautiful.

"Ellen," I said, "this is your hard work. Not mine. You decide what we should call it."

"How about the Georgellen Club?" she asked.

"Why that?" I asked.

"It's us," she said. "Our names. George and Ellen."

"I know, I was teasing. It's wonderful," I said, and hugged her. "What's that?"

We walked closer. It was the sketch of my apartment I had drawn on the grocery bag several years before, hanging over the bar.

Ellen knew the restaurant business. I didn't. I followed

her like a puppy. She hired. She ordered food and furnishings. I learned from her. We were on a tight budget so, initially, we hired two fulltime cooks and two waitresses. When Ellen wasn't managing the club she was waitressing along with the other girls. I was a glorified gofer but it was fine by me. I didn't want to do anything that could mess things up. And Ellen was excited. So was I. I couldn't recall being this happy.

I was a good student of Ellen. Eventually I learned the business, and then things really took off. Some nights were so busy we couldn't keep up. It was all Ellen. She was the creative one of us. I began to see that. I could tell she had a vision that went beyond the Georgellen Club.

"Let's visit," she said one day. I was certain it was about adding a new wing to the club.

We sat at a table in the empty club prior to opening. I had learned to listen to Ellen.

"What is it ?" I asked.

Ellen, as she always did, cut right to the chase. "I'm pregnant" she said.

I'd never really considered having kids. I came from a stable family — two parents, my sisters and me. But I was sneaking up on thirty-five years old, and had led a free spirited life. I might not have it in me to stay with Ellen long term, and a child would tie me down.

"You don't seem too excited," she remarked.

"I don't know how to take it," I said.

"Well, let me help you," she said. "I'm having this child. If I figured you for anything, it was backbone. I won't spend my life with a guy who doesn't show up. And by the way, you're going to be a parent. How you respond is up to you. I know what kind of parent and wife I'm going to be and that would be a good one."

So, having my ass chewed out by Ellen, and realizing that it was time for me to grow up, and that life wasn't all about me, I said, "OK, Ellen, we can do this. You can count on me. But it might be rough sailing for a while."

Ellen looked around the Georgellen Club. "Did you ever think we could do something like this?"

"No, honestly, I didn't," I said.

"And what's my motto?" she asked.

"Dream big, plan well, execute in detail, and come what may," I answered.

"Good, then," she said, "but I want one more thing from you."

"What?" I asked.

She held out her left hand. "I want a ring and the marriage that goes with it. No child of mine will be raised without a real marriage behind it."

So, we got married. And fast. Two weeks later we were in front of a justice of the peace promising that only death would split us up. Ellen took the marriage certificate to the Galveston County Clerk (it never occurred to me those things were actually made public) and we were Mr. and Mrs. George Jax.

We had our child. I sort of figured on a boy thinking that the universe envisioned me as a mentor, teaching George, Jr. how to work on motorcycles, chase girls, or maybe become a professional ball player. (I had absolutely no athletic ability but somewhere back in my gene pool or in Ellen's their might just be such potential.)

But the universe had a different view of things and we had a girl, a fat little thing that looked like me. We named her Julia. Seeing a small version of myself rid me of any concern over the gender of the child. I saw her as my future. My attachment to the girl caught me off guard. I had assumed that Ellen and Julia would bond and that I would play the role of a dutiful father. I couldn't have been more wrong. I spoiled her rotten.

I turned forty-five. We had settled into a comfortable

pattern. Ellen normally opened the club in the morning while I stayed at home with Julia. From noon until 4:00 p.m. I ran the club and Ellen came home. The three of us ate dinner as a family, and then I went back to the club until closing. We made good money. Things went smoothly for several years. Then disaster hit. I had made the mistake of being happy.

Ellen came home one day from the club feeling achy. We figured it for a cold or the flu. She stayed in bed that afternoon and the next day while I covered at the club. Two mornings later she felt fine and went about her routine. However, whatever had her came back a few days later. This time bed rest didn't help. Her body continued to ache and she felt progressively weak. We were not people who practiced preventive medicine. We finally went to the doctor. A few days later the word "terminal" came up in our visit with the doctor. Ellen had acute leukemia. It ate her alive. She was dead inside sixty days.

Until then, there wasn't a death I couldn't get past. But this was different. I went numb. I had crazy regretful thoughts, among them wishing I'd been killed that night in the convenience store robbery instead of facing this. I buried Ellen and did the best I could to make sense of it for Julia.

I had two choices: I could wallow in self-pity or I could push on. I said my goodbyes to Ellen, pledging to raise Julia with the same fearlessness by which Ellen had lived. It wasn't easy. Julia was raised by a series of nannies, all of them properly vetted. Julia, a talkative child, became a silent, pensive teenager.

"Why" she said one night at dinner, "would anyone in their right mind trust life?"

From a girl barely sixteen I could fathom no such question.

"I can't answer that," I said, "because I don't. May I offer you some advice?"

Julia nodded.

"Live life fully. The best revenge against death is good

living."

I threw myself into my business. Ellen's mantra became mine: Dream big, plan well, execute thoroughly, come what may. Within a short period, I opened four new clubs, two in Houston and two along the Gulf Freeway. I did it mostly as a distraction and to honor the spirit of Ellen. I was a good businessman, duly diligent, but I didn't worry about whether the clubs would succeed or not. But they did. I had some sort of Midas touch. Everything I touched turned to wealth. I could not have conceived thirty years ago driving heavy machinery that life would turn into this. Most men would be happy, but I wanted to die knowing that I had raised Julia properly and provided for her future.

That's when I hired Tom York. My parents were dead and my sisters and I had long since lost touch. Two were estranged from me and the other I had never developed much of a relationship with in the first place. (I learned she had come through Houston once and had not bothered to call me.) And Ellen's only brother was, by her description, a black sheep who had wandered off into a world of drugs and alcohol years ago. I had no one to look after Julia. I hired Tom, not thinking of him as a solution to my problem, but as a manager for the Georgellen Club. He came to work for me from a bar in southwest Houston. I valued loyalty above all else and was constantly looking for it in the people around me. Tom was that. Eventually, he ran all my clubs. With his attention to the job, I had more time to spend with Julia.

Then I had my first heart attack. I was fifty-two and had lived life hard. I smoked and drank freely, paying no attention to diet or exercise. I lived life as I had suggested that night to Julia at dinner: fully, freely, with what pleased me now. The future was simply not there. I collapsed one day at the Georgellen Club while chatting with Tom York. One minute I was talking business, intermittently daydreaming about the piece of art that I had drawn many years before and that still hung above the bar. The next thing I knew I was in the ER of John Sealy Hospital. I owed my life to Tom York who had sprung from behind the bar and had started CPR.

I recovered, but it made me all the more determined to find a suitable surrogate for me in Julia's life. She was nineteen and fiercely independent, but, due to the sheltering I had wrapped her in, terribly naïve and lonely. She was a little chick in a wolf's world.

I gambled on Tom. He had worked for me just shy of a decade, and I assessed him as a man of undying loyalty, who lived by a personal code, and whose word was steel. I made him my offer.

"Tom, I owe you my life," I said as we sat at the bar in the Georgellen Club.

"You owe me nothing," he said. "You've been fair to me. I treat people the way they treat me."

"What if," I said, "I was to leave you the Georgellen Club?"

"I don't follow," he said.

From there I explained my situation with Julia. That in exchange for ownership of the club, he would be the trustee of a trust I would set up for Julia and be an informal guardian to her. My belief in him would be our only bond.

"Tom, I expect you to shepherd Julia, to protect her short of nothing."

He sighed, leaning back in his chair. "Short of nothing?" he asked.

"Nothing," I answered.

Our eyes met as we shook hands. I felt a current pass between us.

And then I died. Not at that moment, but a few years later. I was walking on the beach, admiring a sunrise, when I saw a tall young man approaching me. I had begun walking at the advice of my doctors and I loved the peace the mornings brought. For such a beautiful day the beach was strangely absent of people. Normally I would see joggers or lovers walking hand in hand. Not this day. The man came closer, smiling radiantly. He was tall, well over six feet, dressed in baggy shorts and a tee shirt. His hair was blond and the breeze, once salty, now had the sweet aroma of flowers.

"Beautiful day shaping up, eh George?"

I didn't answer immediately. I didn't know him personally. I thought we may have met at the club. I had made many a casual acquaintance over the years. He pointed to the rising sun.

"Out there, George. Out there."

I looked at the orange circle rising above the smooth calm Gulf water. I turned to answer him.

"Yes, it …," I said, but before I could finish my sentence he was gone. There was no one on the beach but me. "Where'd you go?" I asked. And then I looked down. Someone was lying on the ground. It was me. I knew instantly I had seen my last sunrise amongst the living.

So, there it is. I am a ghost. I walk the Georgellen Club. I keep hoping that Ellen will come through here. I have no idea how long this will last. Imagine getting up in the night and walking down the hall to your bathroom so as to relieve yourself. You walk into the bathroom and your nightshirt, dragging behind you, gets stuck in the door, now closed tightly, you're unable to open it. You can't finish your business at the toilet, and you can't go back to your bed. I am trapped between two worlds. And perhaps it is only God, or that fellow who met me on the beach, who can send me to my final destination.